WITCHY ORDERS

WITCHES OF SHADOW LANE MYSTERY BOOK 2

MISTY BANE

Witchy Orders

Witches of Shadow Lane Paranormal Cozy Mystery Series Book 2

Witchy Orders © 2019 by Misty Bane

CONTENTS

"*A*unt Hattie, you can't curse the mailman." My sister, Kiki, flipped her blonde hair over her shoulder with a pointed look and rested her arms on the dining room table.

"The hell I can't." Aunt Hattie scooted forward in her chair and jabbed a finger in Kiki's direction, the sombrero on her head tilting to the side. "He never delivers my packages, and then he lies about it and says I wasn't home. I'm too old to drive down to the post office every other day."

My dad snickered from his seat on the other side of Kiki. "Aunt Hattie, you are not too old. In fact, you're always telling us how *not* old you are."

Aunt Hattie was my father's aunt, and she'd raised him and his sister after their parents had passed. As for my siblings and I, she'd served as both a pseudo-grandmother and, after our own mom ran off, a pseudo-mother as well.

"Fine," she snapped, "but I don't have time for it. Who has time to go to the post office that much? I'm busy." She reached across the table and scooped a heaping spoonful of taco meat onto her plate.

"He's just scared to come down past the graveyard is all," Kiki said. "Lots of folks don't like it. Plus, we run the only funeral home on the island and our last name is Graves. We're also a family of outcast witches with a history of refusing to join a coven. That takes the creepy factor up an extra level or two."

I had no idea why Kiki was taking up for the mailman, but she was going to lose this battle. Aunt Hattie never lost an argument. If she couldn't win with logic, she'd take an alternate route.

My sister-in-law, Paige, piped up from the other end of the table, a mischievous grin on her face. "Kiki went on a date with him a few nights ago."

Kiki narrowed her eyes at Paige. "That's not even relevant."

"Sure it is," Matt, my twin brother, said, agreeing with his wife.

"No, it isn't." Aunt Hattie waved a dismissive hand. "We all know she'll be done with him before we even learn his name."

"Be nice," my dad warned, scowling a little.

"That is nice." Aunt Hattie cocked an eyebrow. "You should hear what I was really thinking."

I cast a sidelong glance at my daughter, Ember, and caught the amused look on her face. We'd only been back in my hometown of Mystic Key for a couple of months, and she'd surprised me with how quickly she'd settled into life on a paranormal island. Even more so, how well she'd adapted to the craziness that was my family.

"Look, Kiki, if I want to curse somebody, I'm going to curse them. Mind your own business." Aunt Hattie sat back in her chair and adjusted the tiny sombrero on my orange tabby cat, Steve's, head. Even though he was *my* cat, Aunt Hattie liked to haul him around in a baby carrier.

"What's with the sombreros, anyway?" I asked.

"Really, Shay? It's taco night. What a daft question." Steve responded in a sardonic tone.

"Oh, of course. How silly of me to question why my cat is wearing a tiny sombrero." I responded back with as much sarcasm as I could muster.

"I just think you're being irrational." Kiki continued to poke the bear, and I considered pinching the back of her arm like I used to do when we were kids.

Aunt Hattie didn't say anything; she simply held up her fork in front of one eye and closed the other.

I was almost afraid to ask, but curiosity got the better of me. "What are you doing?"

Aunt Hattie continued to squint through the silver prongs of her fork. "When Kiki makes me mad, I like to pretend she's in jail."

"How's the miniatures going, Paige?" Bev, my stepmom, attempted to change the subject. She and my dad had married when I was in high school and, while it had taken me a while to warm up to her as a parental figure thanks to my own deadbeat mother, Bev's sweet, nurturing soul made it hard not to love her.

Matt visibly stiffened at Bev's question, and I wondered what exactly that was all about.

"Oh, fabulously!" Paige beamed. "I'm working on creating our family now. I'm almost done with Dad and then I'm moving on to Shay."

Paige liked to take up various hobbies in brief and intense spurts. She would be obsessive about them for a while before dropping them like a hot rock. Most recently, she'd become infatuated with creating tiny miniature scenes that were as realistic as possible. It was actually kind of cool, but it took a lot of patience, precision, and a steady hand — none of which I possessed. I was much better at working on dead bodies.

"Well, I'll be excited to see it then," Bev said in her usual cheerful Southern drawl.

"Yeah, I think I've finally found my thing," Paige continued. "I'm enjoying it so much."

"I thought yoga was your thing?" Aunt Hattie asked before shoving a salsa-drenched chip in her mouth.

"Oh, it is," Paige said with an excited nod, "but I need a creative outlet too, you know?"

Aunt Hattie cackled. "How many hobbies have you gone through now? You're as bad with hobbies as Kiki is with men."

Kiki shot a glare at Aunt Hattie and I gave her a sympathetic pat on the leg. Kiki tried, she really did, but she had some commitment issues—thanks, Mom—and she tended to fall for the wrong types.

"It just takes a while to find the right one," Paige said curtly.

Matt rolled his eyes, and I was dying to know what was going on in his head. I studied him, trying to see if I could get a feel for what he was thinking. As twins—witch twins, no less— we had always had a strong psychic connection when we were kids. Since I hadn't been home in over fifteen years, our connection had faded, and not just the telepathic one.

He pulled his phone from his pocket, and after checking to see who was calling, he answered in his policeman voice. "This is Graves."

The chatter around the table died down since we all assumed it was a work call.

"Yeah, all right. I'll head over." He shook his head and ended the call before he scooted his chair back to stand. "Well, I've gotta go."

"Is everything okay?" Paige asked.

"Yeah. Moira Meeks called in again."

"Moira Meeks? Isn't she the elf that keeps telling everyone around town that she's got a peeping tom?" Kiki asked.

Matt chuckled. "That's her. She's called in everyday for the last few nights, but she can't give us a description and there's no evidence at all. Not a single footprint. Nothing. I think she might be losing it, to tell you the truth." Matt bent down and planted a quick kiss on his wife's cheek before doing the same to both of his children. "I'll be home soon."

"Have fun!" I called out after him. He shot me an annoyed look, and I gave him a playful wink. No matter how old we were, I never got tired of teasing my brother.

"So, what time do we have to be at the Business Leaders thing tomorrow?" Kiki asked me, her eyes glued to the cell phone in her hand.

I let out a deep breath and slouched in my chair. My dad had cajoled me into attending the Business Leaders of Mystic Key networking event on behalf of the Graves' Funeral Home and Crematorium. I wasn't the owner; I was the cosmetologist. And I certainly wasn't the networking, schmoozer type either. I was the type that had specifically chosen to work with dead bodies so I didn't have to deal with live ones all day. Still, my dad had somehow convinced me to go on behalf of the family business, and I had a hard time saying no to him.

Kiki was attending the event because she owned Cosmopoli-Tan, a successful beauty bar in town, but mostly because she wanted to scope out the eligible business owners and have a few cocktails.

"I'll pick you up at six forty-five. It starts at seven," I said before giving her a sharp look and adding, "And don't make us late."

Kiki didn't even look up, instead her gaze was fixed on the glowing screen of her cell phone. Her thumb scrolled so furiously that it was nothing more than a blur.

"Kiki?" I nudged her with my elbow.

"Yeah," she murmured, distracted.

"No phones at the dinner table," my dad said through a mouthful of food.

"Sorry, but this is too good." Kiki grinned and finally looked up. "You know Brock Garrett, right? The wolf shifter that owns Alpha Gym?"

An instantaneous groan filled the dining room.

"Okay, so he's in the middle of an argument with like twenty people on Monster Mash."

"What's Monster Mash?" I asked.

"Shay." Kiki looked at me like I had two heads.

"What?" I whipped my head to the side to look over at Ember.

"It's like Facebook but for paranormals." Ember looked at me with pity for being so obviously out of touch.

"How do you know about it?"

"I'm fifteen." She rolled her eyes and let out a short laugh.

"Touché." I shrugged and turned my attention back to Kiki. "Okay, so what's the gossip?"

"Well, apparently he's been going around town trying to bully some of the townspeople into selling either their buildings or their land to him. He wants to open up a second, bigger gym. And people are … angry."

"He came by here," Aunt Hattie said.

"He did?" My dad wrinkled his brow.

She nodded and fed a spoonful of taco meat to Steve. "I sent him on his way though."

"I guess he met with the Gratz sisters too," Kiki said.

"I'm sure that went over real well." I laughed at the image in my head of someone trying to convince the Gratzes of anything. The Gratz sisters were vampires who owned the Lettuce Inn, a great little bed-and-breakfast just next to the graveyard.

"No, it didn't," Kiki responded, obviously missing my sarcasm. "In fact, Lara is on here really giving it to him. He's such a narcissist though that he thinks what she's really angry about is that he doesn't want to date her." Kiki was almost gleeful.

"Why are you so happy?" Aunt Hattie cocked an eyebrow and eyed her suspiciously.

"Kiki loves drama." I answered.

"I do not," she said, glowering at me.

"Yes, you do. It's evident by your choice in TV shows. You eat stuff like this up. Just look at you. Look at how happy you are right now."

"I find it entertaining." She shrugged and went back to staring at her phone screen.

"I wonder if he'll find someone to sell to him," I thought aloud.

"Not likely." My dad wiped the corners of his mouth with his napkin. "Even if someone around here was looking to sell, they wouldn't sell to him out of sheer principle. The guy has a reputation for being a jerk and a playboy. He doesn't have too many friends."

"And the wolf shifters only tolerate him because they have to," Paige added. "Part of the whole pack-mentality thing."

"Yup, and Ross Burkman is commenting on here and telling Brock to shut up, basically." Kiki said.

Ross Burkman was the wolf shifters' leader and, from what I'd heard, he ran a pretty tight ship. Keeping someone like

Brock Garrett in line was difficult even for an ex-military man like Ross, though.

"Not only that, but this entire post is full of people calling him out for his behavior. It's getting pretty intense. First it was just about the gym stuff, but now people are going after him for the way he treats women." Kiki started taking screen shots with her phone and cast a sidelong glance in my direction. "Just in case. I have a feeling things are only going to get worse."

"Well, the idiot's made his own bed," Aunt Hattie pointed out, reaching for another scoop of taco meat. "Might as well sit back and enjoy the show."

CHAPTER TWO

*K*iki had promised to meet Ember and me outside of Whimsical Wand Emporium at ten the next morning. We'd had it planned for weeks, and I was hoping she hadn't forgotten. I'd managed to snag a parking spot directly in front of Brews Brothers, the local coffee shop, and I glanced up and down the street for my sister's car.

I pulled my cell from my purse and was just about to call her when we rounded the corner, and I spotted my sister chatting it up with a tall, handsome man. He had his back to me, and if it wasn't for the short hair, I would've sworn it was Roman Daniels. Roman was a druid and had such a large, imposing frame that he stood out everywhere he went. He had dark hair that skimmed the top of his shoulders, though, and while this muscleman in front of me was built eerily the same, his hair was cropped into a short crew cut.

Roman and I were friends, and I continued to remind myself of that despite the fact that my heart skipped just a little every time I saw him. Kiki glimpsed in my direction and raised her arm in a friendly wave. The man she'd been talking to turned around and my heart leapt.

I waited until we were just a few feet away before I blurted out, "You cut your hair!"

He grinned and ran his hand over his short new do. "Yeah, it was time. Once it gets long enough, I like to donate it. Then I start the process all over again."

"That's really cool." Ember seemed genuinely impressed.

He smiled down at her. "Your aunt here was just telling me that you're getting your first wand today. That's a big deal. Are you excited?"

Ember nodded enthusiastically. "I've been bugging my mom for months."

"She's exaggerating," I said, shaking my head and shooting her an exasperated look.

"No, I'm not. I asked you about it on my birthday. That was two months ago."

"Yes, but you just got your magic *on* your birthday, and wands are a big step. You don't turn sixteen and run out and drive a car, do you? No, you complete driver's education, you practice, you take a test, you do all of that first."

"You didn't," my loud-mouthed sister cut in. "Remember? You took dad's car out that very day and crashed into The Merry Mechanic?"

"Kiki," I hissed and shot her a warning look.

"Well, you did," she muttered under her breath.

"Anyway, we're here now." I replaced my scowl with a smile and an upbeat tone.

"Are you coming to the networking event later?" Roman asked.

"We are," Kiki answered, even though his eyes were fixed on me.

"Great," he replied with a warm smile. "Maybe we can have some time to chat then? I'll buy you a drink."

"Yeah, okay. Sure, that sounds … that would be nice." I stumbled over my words and felt heat rush to my cheeks.

He said goodbye to each of us, and I attempted to calm the butterflies in my stomach by taking a few steady breaths.

"Shay's got a date," Kiki teased as she bumped my shoulder with hers.

"Stop. It's not a date." I narrowed my eyes at her.

"Mom, he obviously likes you." Ember rolled her eyes.

"Yes, because we're friends," I said adamantly.

"Oh, please, Shay. I don't know who you're trying to convince, but no one here is buying it," Kiki said.

I let out a deep breath. "Look, are we getting a wand today or not?"

"Yes!" Ember said, shooting a look at my sister. "Don't make her mad, Aunt Kiki."

"Fine." Kiki groused.

I pulled open the heavy door and stepped inside, holding it open for Ember and Kiki.

The inside of the wand shop felt like something akin to stepping inside a candy store as a kid. My eye was drawn in so many different directions and the possibilities were over-whelming. I started toward a wall of glitter-infused wands when I realized Ember wasn't next to me. I turned to see her frozen in place, her eyes darting around the store in amaze-ment. I took a moment to take in the scene from her perspective, and it truly was amazing. Hundreds, maybe thousands, of wands of various shapes and sizes and colors lined the walls, and shorter shelving units in the center were dedicated to fairy wands. A small, wiry man in a tight purple suit glided out from behind the counter, the soles of his dress shoes allowing him to slide across the sleek tile floor.

"Good morning," he beamed, "and welcome to Whimsical Wand Emporium. My name is Chester. Is there something I can help you find today?"

"My niece needs her first wand." Kiki said, her voice tinged with pride.

Chester's face lit up in delight at the prospect of helping a new witch find the perfect wand, and he reached out and grabbed Ember by the arm. He began chattering away about style choices and weight and what was best for a novice. Kiki and I hurried to keep up as he pulled Ember along to a section of wands near the back of the store.

"It's best if you hold them in your hand to really get a feel for them," he was saying, "but you also want to choose something that you won't be embarrassed to be seen with."

He reached for a ladder and pulled it to him before he ascended to its midpoint. "All right, my dear." He looked down at Ember gleefully. "Pick your poison."

She studied the options in front of her for a few moments before she spoke. "I'd like to see the green one just to the left of you. And that white one with the stones in the handle." She pointed to a beautiful wand that I was certain I couldn't afford.

"There are no prices listed." I whispered to Kiki.

"I know. It's a sales tactic," she whispered back.

"Excellent choices." Chester said, handing the first wand to Ember. It was rather small but was a beautiful jade color. Shades of blue settled into the deep crevices of wood and were reminiscent of lightning bolts. The handle was modest - a simple black shade with tiny stars etched into the top of the base. Ember twisted it around in her hand and examined it closely before handing it back to Chester.

He offered her the white one, which looked to be made of some kind of stone. The light bounced off its curves as she twisted it in her hand. A row of colorful stones rested just above where she placed her hand, and I had to admit, it was a gorgeous wand.

"Ember, choose whatever you'd like," I said. "You can look at more options too, okay? I just want you to get what you want."

She nodded and looked up at the wall of wands again. "Can I see the green one again?"

Chester, still holding it in his hand, climbed down from the ladder and placed it carefully in her open palm. "You're welcome to try it out. Just to get a feel for it. It hasn't been infused with any magic yet."

Ember held it with a loose grip and tested the weight before grasping it and waving her hand around in the air a few times. Once she was satisfied, she turned to me. "Can I have this one?"

"Are you sure?" I asked, noting the white wand still in Chester's hand. "You can choose whichever one you like. Don't worry about the cost."

"Yeah. I'm pitching in, so get whatever you want." Kiki added.

"Oh, you don't have to do that," I said, but was glad she'd offered.

She rolled her eyes at me and I mouthed a thank you.

"I'm sure." Ember gave a firm nod.

Chester led us back to the front counter, and I attempted to do some mental math as I tried to remember exactly how much I had left in my bank account and on my credit card.

"Wait!" Ember spun around suddenly. "Mom, you need a wand too."

"Oh, no." I stuttered, taken aback. "No, I don't need one today."

Kiki gasped in excitement and bounced up and down. "Yes! Shay doesn't have a wand!"

"I do. I have my old one. I think it's in Dad's attic."

"That one is so old it probably doesn't even work anymore." Kiki waved her hand flippantly. "Chester, what would you recommend for a witch who hasn't used her magic much in the last fifteen years?"

Chester widened his eyes and after a full beat, a grin spread across his face. He took off down the length of the store, letting his shoes glide him between rows of wands. Once I was sure he was out of earshot, I turned to Kiki.

"I can't afford two wands today," I said, keeping my voice low.

"You don't need to," she replied, matching my tone. "I have a credit."

"You do?"

She nodded. "It's old, but Chester will honor it." She gave me a bright smile. "See, nothing to worry about."

I heard the sound of Chester's shoes sliding across the floor again, and suddenly he was at my side. He held out a long case lined with snow-white velvet that contained three wands. I could tell by the way he tipped his chin up that he was rather pleased with himself. "These are not your ordinary wands, miss. In fact, I keep them in the back for such occasions as this."

"What's so special about them?" Ember asked, peering over my shoulder to see inside the case.

"They know how to teach an old dog new tricks." He winked and shoved the case a little closer to me.

I examined the contents and selected the first wand. It was fairly simple aside from the crimson color. It felt a little heavy in my hand though, so I set it back. The middle wand had far too many bells and whistles for my taste, so I skipped right over it. The last one, though, felt like it was calling to me. I plucked it from its warm, velvety home and held it in my hand. It was light enough that I could move my hand with ease, but heavy enough that I wasn't afraid it would float away if I didn't grip it tightly enough. It was white with the slightest hint of blue, and an intricate pattern wound round the band of wood at the top of the handle.

"She has chosen," Chester announced, slamming the case shut victoriously.

We gave our new wands to Chester and waited patiently while he enchanted them. When he was done, I took a deep breath and braced myself for the total. Instead, he handed Ember and I each our wands. "Now, come back and see me if you have any trouble at all. I'm always happy to help."

"Uh, what's the total?" I asked.

He smiled a bit devilishly. "It's been taken care of."

I glanced from Chester to Kiki, but she only offered me a confused look. "It wasn't me."

"Who paid for us?" I asked.

"I promised not to tell." He was still sporting a cheeky grin. "But let's just say I think you have a secret admirer."

"A... what?" I looked back and forth from Kiki to Ember.

Kiki looped her arm through mine and led me to the door. "Thanks, Chester," she called out over her shoulder.

"Wait—" I attempted to protest.

"Mom needs coffee." Ember smirked. "Her brain doesn't work right unless she's had at least four cups in the morning."

"So that's why she's confused." Kiki giggled.

"Can you two not talk about me like I'm not here?" I grumbled.

Ember studied her wand and I blurted out a word of caution. "Put that away! It works now, and you don't have a firm enough grasp on your magic to use it properly just yet. At least not in public."

She rolled her eyes at me and muttered something under her breath.

"Roman, dummy," Kiki said. "He must've given Chester his card or something so he could pay."

"Why? Why would he do that?"

"Because he's nice," Ember said.

"And because he likes you." Kiki added.

"But how did he know we'd be coming today?" Ember still had her wand in her hand and it was making me anxious.

I motioned for her to put her wand in her pocket. "I texted with him a little yesterday and mentioned it. That's why he must've been outside the store when Kiki ran into him."

"Aww. What a sweetheart!" Kiki gushed. "I wish I could find a guy that's so thoughtful."

"You have," I said with a laugh, nudging her in the ribs with my elbow. "You've found lots of them. You just dump them all."

I caught a swirl of blue and purple sparkling out of the corner of my eye and watched as magic shot from Ember's wand. I didn't have time to react before it collided with a woman walking toward us. I recognized her instantly as my neighbor, Lara Gratz, only seconds before she turned into a large pink flamingo.

She shrieked and began to flap her wings violently, and I could see the terror and confusion in her eyes.

I cursed and pointed my wand at her along with Kiki. After a quick spell, Lara was back to her vampire self. She still stood on one leg as she patted at her body in disbelief.

"Lara, I am so sorry." I said, running over to her.

Ember's cheeks were beet red and I noticed she'd finally shoved her wand into her back pocket. "I'm really sorry. It was an accident," she said.

"Oh, of course it was. It's okay. Really." Lara's voice shook, but she attempted a smile.

I shot Ember a glare that I hoped read *I told you so*.

"I have no idea how that even happened," she mused.

"You were messing around with your wand after I told you to put it away. It's dangerous. You can't just flip it around all over town," I scolded.

"Calm down, Shay. It was an accident," Kiki said, but she winced once I fixed my cool gaze on her.

"It's really okay," Lara said, "I mean, it's an interesting way to start the morning, but it's no big deal. Really." She spoke hurriedly and I wasn't sure if she had some place to be or if she just wanted to get as far away from us as possible.

"Where are you off to in such a rush?" I asked. "I promise we won't turn you into any other feathered creatures."

She looked back and forth between the three of us before letting out a prolonged sigh. "I'm actually on my way to the police station."

"The police station? Is everything okay?"

"No. No, it's not." She crossed her arms over her chest and jutted her hip out. "I'm sick of Brock Garrett and his crap, and I'm going to file an official complaint."

I swear I could feel the squeal of delight emanating from somewhere deep inside Kiki even though she fought to subdue it.

"Oh, yeah," Kiki said with an effort to keep her tone casual. "I think I saw something on Monster Mash. Some folks are pretty upset about the way he's going around trying to force people into selling their land to him. Is that right?"

I resisted the urge to groan and roll my eyes at her poor display of nonchalance.

"That's the gist," Lara said. "He's nothing but a bully, and I'm not going to let him push me around. He thinks just because we had a ... a thing that he has some leverage over me—"

"Wait." Kiki held up her hand. "You really did have a thing with Brock Garrett?"

Lara's cheeks turned a light shade of pink. "Yes. It was stupid. One of those onetime rebound things." She let out a nervous laugh.

"Oh, I know all about those, honey." Kiki waved a hand in the air.

"We all do," I added.

"Well, he's one of those rebounds that you regret with every fiber of your being," Lara continued. "He thinks I'm in love with him or something, and he keeps coming by the inn and trying to use that to convince me to sell half of our land to him. I want to report him for harassment and hopefully get a restraining order."

"Wow. It must've been a really bad one-night stand," I muttered.

"You have no idea." She sighed. "And, as a warning, he's very charming when he wants to be, so be prepared. I'm sure he'll stop by your place too."

"He already has. He met Aunt Hattie though, so I doubt he'll be back." I told her.

"Good then." She adjusted her purse strap. "Will I see you two at the networking event tonight?"

"We'll be there," I said.

"Great. See you then." She gave us a little wave before she went on her way.

"Do you think Brock will be there too?" Kiki asked.

"Oh, I'd bet on it."

She finally let out the squeal of delight she'd been holding back. "Yes! Those meetings are always so boring."

"Well, I have a feeling we'll get a decent show tonight."

CHAPTER THREE

Mystic Key had exactly one swanky bar. As such, the staff and regular patrons liked to tip their chins just a bit higher in the air when they referred to it as a cocktail lounge. As for me, I thought the drinks were overpriced and there was a severe lack of seating. I hated standing and avoided it like the plague. However, Kiki had taken an excruciatingly long time getting her eyeliner just right for the occasion, and we'd made it to Top Shelf just in time to watch a group of elves commandeer the last table.

I shot Kiki an annoyed look. "You're paying for my drinks tonight."

She recoiled and widened her eyes. "*All* of them?"

"Yes, all of them. And I don't have to work tomorrow, so I hope you're prepared."

She smirked and looped her arm through mine as we walked up to the bar. "You think that's a punishment, but I don't even mind. You need to have some fun. Loosen up a little. And tipsy Shay is fun Shay."

"Hey, I'm fun without alcohol." I protested.

She shrugged and leaned her elbows on the bar. "If you say so."

"Kiki!" I poked her in the ribs.

"I'm kidding." She laughed and wriggled away, and I caught her checking to see if the good-looking man fairy behind the bar was watching.

"Since when do you go for fairies?" I leaned in and asked in a low voice.

"Since they look like that." She grinned and turned her attention back to the bartender who was giving her a flirty smile.

I groaned and turned around so I didn't have to watch their exchange. I rested my back against the bar and surveyed the room, looking for familiar faces.

It was my first Business Leaders of Mystic Key event, and I realized that it was just like any other networking event I'd ever been to. There were the schmoozers working the room, the introverts pretending to be deeply invested in something on their cell phones, and the people who were already two drinks in trying desperately to feel comfortable socializing with strangers.

I spotted Lara Gratz deep in conversation with her sister, Gretchen. The Gratzs were as different as sisters could get. Lara was tall with platinum hair, and delicate features. She was the most reserved of the three sisters, but if you paid close enough attention, it was obvious that she ran the show. Gretchen was nearly as tall, but she rocked a much larger frame and always wore her vibrant red hair up in a messy bun or braid. I didn't see Mina in attendance, but that fact didn't surprise me. The Inn had never been of much interest to her, and she had a habit of complaining about every aspect of the business.

Kiki held out a tall glass layered with orange and red liquid and topped off with a spear of cherries. A puddle of dark rum settled on top.

"This looks dangerous." I said, taking the drink from her.

"It is."

I sipped a bit of the cold drink through the straw and a burst of tropical flavors invaded my mouth. "What is this?"

"Don't ask," Kiki advised.

"Well, whatever it is, it's heavenly."

"Exactly. Don't drink more than two, though, or I'll have to carry you out of here."

"Good evening, ladies." A strikingly handsome man approached us and offered a polite smile. His pale skin and long hair were nearly the same color, and both were a notice-able contrast to his deep red suit. I quickly glanced at his nametag and felt like an idiot for not realizing who he was sooner.

"Good evening, Mayor Valentine." My father had always taught us the value of having a firm handshake, and I figured offering a hand that was wet from the condensation on my glass wasn't a great look. I wiped my hand on the front of my dress and reached out to give him my best handshake.

"It's so nice to see you here mingling with the peasants." Kiki placed her hand on his bicep and let out a girlish laugh. I fought the urge to roll my eyes at her blatant attempt to flirt.

"I don't consider any of the townspeople peasants." He furrowed his brow. "I grew up in Italy during the middle ages. I can assure you, Mystic Key has no peasants."

I stifled my laughter as Kiki's cheeks grew an obvious shade of red. "Well it's nice to see you here all the same."

"How are you settling in?" I asked. Alister Valentine had recently taken over as Mystic Key's new mayor. The old one was rotting away in a jail cell after killing the last two high priestesses of the witch council.

"Quite well. Thank you for asking," he replied a bit stiffly. I'd seen him around a few times and I was still trying to get a read on him. Vampires—specifically the old school ones—were a strange breed. Most of them had been around for centuries, and they had literally seen it all. As a result, they always appeared stoic and disaffected.

"Well, I, for one, am so happy that we found such a capable person to take over." Kiki was still attempting to flatter him.

"I appreciate that, miss." He stuffed his hands in his suit pockets and looked between us. "I do hope you ladies enjoy your evening." He glanced around awkwardly before wandering around to the side of the bar.

Kiki had already turned her attention back to the bartender even though she still had a full drink. I decided to leave her to her own devices and do some mingling. I scanned the crowd for Lara again, but I didn't see her or Gretchen anywhere. I did, however, spot Glenda White. Glenda had recently taken over as the High Priestess of the Witch Council. She also owned a successful law firm in town. At present, however, she was in the midst of a conversation with a man, and I could tell by the way her eyes darted around that she was looking for an escape. She caught my eye and waved eagerly.

I let out a small breath and made my way over.

"Shay, hi!" She pulled me in for a grateful hug. "Have you met Brock Garrett yet?"

"No. Shay Graves." I shook his hand and the first thing I noticed was how hairy his knuckles were. The second thing I noticed was that he looked like every Frat boy, meathead I'd ever met. It was as if they lined up in a factory and everything about them that made them unique, interesting human beings oozed out the sides of the mold they were pressed in.

"Graves?" He flashed me a bright white smile and, had he been a cartoon character, I was certain a gleam of light would've bounced off his teeth along with the appropriate sound effect.

I nodded in response, forcing my eyes to stop wandering down to get another look at his shaggy knuckles.

"So, you own the funeral business up on Shadow Lane then?"

"It's a family business."

"I see. I was under the impression that an older woman owned it." He scratched his chin. "Helen, I think her name was."

"Hattie." I corrected. "My aunt. No, technically my father owns it."

"Hmm. I went to speak with the owner just last week, but Helen acted as if it was her business."

"Hattie." I corrected again.

"Sorry?"

"Her name is Hattie. You keep calling her Helen."

"Oh, sorry. I'm not very good with names." He grinned and gave me a once-over, and a shiver ran down my spine. "Anyway, the reason I went by was that I was hoping to speak with the owner about buying some of the land. You all have so much up there that's unused."

"Well, it's unused for now. But it's a graveyard. Unless you've got a potion for immortality—" I joked.

"Vampires." He said flatly.

"What?"

"Vampires. They're immortal."

I glanced at Glenda, whose face read just as confused as mine must have.

"I know they're immortal. What's your point?"

"Well, you said if I had a potion for immortality, then the land would remain unused. And, while it's not a potion, it's a solution."

"Wait ..." I tried to wrap my mind around what he was implying. "So, you're saying that we need to turn the rest of the town into vampires so you can buy the unused land at the graveyard."

He shrugged, a grin tugging at the corner of his mouth. "It's worth thinking about."

"What?" I shook my head, hoping to rid my brain of the stupid that he had just injected me with.

"Brock." An older man joined us, slapping Brock just a little too hard on the back. He grimaced as his drink sloshed up over the rim of his glass and splattered onto his white polo.

"Better get some seltzer water on that," Glenda advised.

Brock muttered something under his breath before excusing himself to visit the bar.

"Thanks, Ross." Glenda let out a relieved sigh.

"I didn't spill his drink on him on purpose." Ross chuckled.

"I know. But I appreciate the interruption."

He nodded in understanding and reached out to shake my hand. "I don't believe we've met. I'm Ross Burkman."

"Of course. Shay Graves."

"It's nice to meet you, Shay. I've heard a lot about you. I hope Brock wasn't bothering you." His eyes slid toward the bar.

"He has some interesting ideas." I cocked an eyebrow at Glenda, and she smirked in response.

"He's …" Ross let out a deep sigh and shrugged. "I do what I can."

"I get it," I said. "I have a cat with an aversion to baths."

Ross chuckled and tipped his glass in my direction. "That's spot on."

"Excuse me." Glenda said suddenly, placing a light hand on my arm. "I see someone I need to talk to."

"Sure." I replied, watching her weave through the sea of people. I was hoping to see who she was so intent on talking with, but I lost her behind a hulking man engrossed in conversation with a gray-haired elf. My stomach flipped at the sight of Roman and I ignored it by turning my attention back to Ross.

"So, Ross, what do you do?" I said, putting my drink to my lips. I'd need about three more of them if I was going to enjoy mindless chatter.

"I own Brews Brothers. It's a coffee shop downtown."

"Oh, I love that place! I didn't realize you were the owner."

A sheepish smile spread across his face. "Thank you. I don't spend as much time there as I'd like these days since I'm opening up a second coffee shop."

"Oh, really? In Mystic Key?"

He nodded. "Just on the other side of town. It won't be ready for a few more weeks." He appeared distracted by something behind me and he motioned with his glass. "In fact, there's my business partner. Craig!"

I looked back over my shoulder to see an attractive man walking toward us. He wore a fitted dress shirt and slacks, and his tan skin conflicted with the vampire fangs I noticed when he smiled.

"Shay Graves, this is my business partner, Craig Baldwin."

"Wonderful to meet you, Shay." Craig gave me a slight nod and shook my hand. "Graves as in the Graves' Funeral Home?"

"That's the one."

"Oh, lovely." Craig smiled, but a darkness suddenly crept over his features. "That's right next to the Lettuce Inn, isn't it?"

"Yes. The Gratz sisters have been our neighbors for years."

"I see. Well, I offer my condolences." He looked away and let his gaze dance around the dimly lit bar.

"Uh, Craig doesn't get along well with the Gratzes." Ross explained.

"Yes, there's no love lost there." Craig mused with a lopsided grin. "Though they've recently been hoisted from their position at the top of my list."

"Oh?" I was intrigued.

"Brock Garrett." He let the words out through clenched teeth.

"It seems he's making the rounds lately," I said.

"He's been trying to convince Craig to sell the new space we just purchased for Java the Hut."

"Java the Hut? The new coffee shop?"

"Yeah. That or close down Brews Brothers and let him buy that spot." Ross shook his head. "I just ignore him, but Craig …" his voice trailed off.

"He's hard to ignore when he spreads rumors behind your back and smiles in your face." Craig rocked back on his heels and stuffed his free hand in his pocket.

"I know the type," I replied, my tone dry.

A commotion from the front of the bar interrupted our conversation, and I did my best to peer around the other onlookers. Lara was shoving her finger in Brock's face and yelling obscenities while he threw his head back in raucous laughter.

"I'd better break that up." Ross handed me his drink and headed for the front of the bar.

"I'm not sure why he tries to look out for him." Craig stood next to me as we both surveyed the scene. "Brock's only going to learn if he gets what's coming to him once in a while."

"I don't disagree, but I think it has something to do with the whole pack mentality thing." I took the opportunity to chug the rest of my drink. I figured Craig wouldn't be one to judge me over it, and the smile he gave me proved my theory correct.

More shouting tore my eyes away from Craig and I saw Gretchen pulling Lara toward the front door. The two bickered in hushed whispers and struggled against each other. I strained to hear what they were saying but I couldn't make anything out. At least, not until they brushed past me and I heard Gretchen whisper, "You couldn't control yourself for one night?"

I looked back to Brock, who was already immersed in conversation with a chesty blonde who laughed a little too hard at something he said.

Ross made his way back to us and ran a hand through his hair in frustration. I handed him his drink, which he gladly put to his lips.

"This was much more eventful than most of these things." Craig smirked. "Though they should've let her finish him off."

He sipped on his drink and the light glinted off the tip of his fang. An involuntary shudder ran through me. Vampires weren't scary, blood-sucking creatures anymore, but the fact that they still had the ability to be made me a little wary of them sometimes.

Kiki was suddenly at my side, gripping my arm. "Holy shifter, did you see that?"

"Yeah, I've never seen Lara that angry before. She's always so calm and collected."

Craig snickered and pursed his lips for a full beat before he spoke. "I'm not sure her exes would agree."

"Really?" Kiki leaned in, prepared to soak up any gossip Craig wanted to offer her.

"Wow," Ross said, finally having downed the rest of his cocktail. "That was really tense."

"You think that was tense?" I heard a voice, but it wasn't coming from anyone in my circle. "Try being stalked. That's tense."

I looked down to find a small woman, her arms crossed angrily over her chest as she scowled up at each of us.

"Oh, hello Miss. Meeks." Ross smiled down at her.

"Did you say someone is being stalked?" I asked.

"Not someone. Me." She jabbed her finger into her chest. Her jaw jutted out and it left her with a severe under-bite, though I ventured to guess that she would've been making an angry face, regardless.

"You're being stalked?" Craig sounded amused.

"Darn right I am. And the cops couldn't give a flying pig's butt." She spat the words. "I've called them three times now. You'd think they'd at least leave a patrol car out or something, but they don't care. They think I'm crazy, but I'm not crazy! I've seen them sneaking around."

"Who?" Ross asked.

"Well, if I knew that then we'd be having a different conversation!" She barked, spittle flying from her lips.

"Calm down, Moira." Craig rolled his eyes and sipped on his crimson drink. I hadn't realized it before, but he was definitely drinking blood. Well, the synthetic variety, anyway.

"I am calm. You should see me when I'm not calm," she exclaimed, though she'd subdued her tone to that of a petulant child. She adjusted her glasses and opened her mouth to say something else when a familiar scent permeated my senses.

It was a mixture of a summer evening and a hint of the

forest after a light rain. I looked up to see Roman standing inches from me, and despite the large group surrounding me, he had his gaze fixed intently on me. A kaleidoscope of butterflies took flight in my stomach at the exact second Kiki reached down and gave my free hand a knowing squeeze.

"I hope I'm not interrupting," he said in his smooth, deep voice.

"No, not at all. Moira was just telling us about her stalker." Kiki answered.

"Oh?" Roman knelt a bit to look down at Moira, since the top of her head barely reached his waist.

"You don't need to bend down to speak to me. I can hear you just fine," she grumbled.

"He's not trying to offend you," I told her.

"Well, he is. You don't squat down to talk to a short person. It's impolite."

"Well, I'm short too, and I have never heard that before," I argued.

"You know what?" Moira gave us each a pointed look over the top of her glasses before her gaze landed on me. "I'm going home."

And with that, she turned on her heels and stomped away. Craig burst into laughter and she shot him a glare over her shoulder.

"Everyone's a bit … on edge this evening, it seems." Roman raised his eyebrows.

"I know. It's Brock. He's really created a tense environment, and everyone is just feeding off of it and reacting to all the negative energy," Kiki said.

I scrunched my brow and looked at her.

She lifted a shoulder. "What? I've been reading a book about energies."

"Is it *Awaken* by Edmund Cromwell?" Craig asked.

Kiki's eyes widened. "It is. Have you read it?"

He nodded excitedly. "I was great friends with Edmund. In fact, I helped him with his research."

"No way!" Kiki beamed. "I'd love to talk to you about it." She smiled shyly and crossed her arms in a way that pushed her cleavage together. It was a typical Kiki move, and I'd seen it a thousand times.

"Need another drink?" I asked Roman.

He looked down at his glass, still nearly full, and then to mine. "No, but it looks like you do."

"Ross?" I asked, not wanting to leave him alone with Kiki and Craig during their flirt fest.

"No, I'm all right. I think I'm going to go chat with Matthias Sharpe though. We have some business to discuss." He gave us a polite smile before wandering away.

"So, I do have something to talk with you about." I kept my eyes on the floor in an effort to avoid slipping on any potential spilled liquid and falling on my face.

"What's that?" he asked, his arm brushing against mine as he stuffed his hand in his pocket.

We reached the bar and I set my empty glass down. The bartender was busy helping Brock, so I turned my attention back to Roman. "I know it was you."

"Sorry?" He cocked his head to the side.

"You had Chester let you pay for our wands today."

"Oh, no. I think you're confused."

"I'm not confused," I protested.

"Lovers' quarrel?" Brock appeared between us and the overwhelming smell of alcohol exuded from his pores and wafted through the air.

"No. But this is a private conversation," I said, trying to breathe through my mouth.

"Oh, yeah? How private? Like he's in trouble or like you want him to follow you into the bathroom?" He snickered and stumbled forward.

"Hey." Roman narrowed his eyes and stepped closer to me.

"Go away," I said in a firm tone.

"Oh, pardon me." He laughed and held up his hands defensively. "Got yourself a feisty one, huh?" he asked Roman, jabbing his thumb in my direction and swaying slightly. "I like 'em feisty too. They might be a little crazy, but they are good in—"

"All right." Roman placed a firm grip on Brock's shoulder and he hunched forward with a wince. "That's enough. The lady told you once. Don't make her tell you again," he growled.

Brock widened his bloodshot eyes and nodded, and once Roman released him, he scampered away, bumping into everyone he passed.

Roman's expression softened and he placed his hand lightly on my arm. "I'm sorry. Are you okay?"

I shrugged, noncommittal. "Yeah, I'm fine. He's not the first drunk creep to cross my path, and I doubt he'll be the last."

"Still. You shouldn't be treated that way." He looked concerned, and I felt a little guilty at how much I liked that he had stood up for me. I had always been independent, even during my marriage to Scott, and I prided myself on handling jerks on my own. My guard was slipping, that much I knew, and it made me uncomfortable.

"Good on ya, brother!" The gray-haired elf that Roman had been talking to earlier hobbled toward us, his eyes fixed on Roman. I recognized Morty Mortenson right away, but I was hopeful that it wouldn't be reciprocated.

Once he reached us, he looked at me and the smile on his face fell away. He squinted and after a moment he asked, "You're Alvin Graves' daughter, ain't ya?"

I wondered if I could get away with pretending to be Kiki, but Roman messed it up when he said, "You know Shay?"

The elf stared at me a moment longer, and I shifted uncomfortably from one foot to the other.

His eyes slid over to Roman and he screwed up his face. "She drove a car through my auto repair shop once."

"Ha, yeah." I grimaced, fidgeting nervously with the straw in my empty glass. "It's funny, my sister just mentioned that earlier today."

"It was quite the scene. Cost a lot of money to clean that mess up." He eyed me and it was obvious that he hadn't gotten over the whole thing.

"I remember. My dad made me work to pay it off. Sorry, again, Mr. Mortenson." I suddenly felt sixteen again, apologizing for a stupid accident that had happened because I was too stubborn and impulsive to do things the right way.

"Teenagers, right?" Roman laughed in an obvious effort to ease the tension. "You know, Morty, I saw that old mustang parked outside your shop when I drove by today. Is that yours?"

Morty's eyebrows lifted, and a look of delight played across his features. He launched into a long-winded story about the mustang, and I pretended to listen while he and Roman chatted.

I scanned the crowd, looking for Brock Garrett, but it seemed he had left for good. After what felt like an eternity of car talk, Morty finally wandered off, leaving me alone with Roman again. Just as I was about to bring up the wands, the bartender interrupted.

"What can I get you?" He placed his hands on the bar and leaned forward to hear us over the noise. I opted for a martini this time while Roman went with a beer. Once the bartender placed the drinks in front of us, I resumed the discussion I'd been waiting impatiently to have.

"So, the wands," I said.

"What wands?" He put his beer mug to his lips but I saw a sparkle of mischief in his eyes.

"Roman, you didn't have to do that—"

"Do what?" he asked.

"Stop. I know it was you. And, honestly, you really … you didn't need to buy our wands."

"You're right. I didn't need to." He let his eyes move around the room, escaping eye contact with me. "I wanted to."

I was embarrassed that I hadn't known he'd be paying and spent more than I would have otherwise, but I was even more embarrassed that I didn't know how to properly express my gratitude. "It's not that I'm not grateful—"

His gaze darted back in my direction and his brow was set in a hard line. "By the way, I only meant to pay for Ember's wand. I had no idea you'd be treating yourself on my dime." My stomach lurched and I felt a wave of heat reach my cheeks. I moved my mouth, but no sound came out.

After an agonizing few seconds, he finally winked and let out a deep belly laugh. "I'm teasing! I told Kiki to make sure you picked one out for yourself too."

"Kiki?"

"Yeah, when I ran into her this morning out front. I let her know I'd given Chester my card and told her to make sure you didn't leave the store without one too."

"Why that little …" I spotted Kiki in a corner of the bar flirting with a new guy who I didn't recognize. I narrowed my eyes at her and I was certain she felt my glare when her gaze flicked briefly in my direction. No wonder she'd been so pushy about making sure I picked a wand for myself. Usually, I could see through Kiki's stories like swiss cheese, but I was impressed with her acting skills in this instance.

"Look, I'd like to pay you back." I opened my purse with the full knowledge that I didn't have any cash on me and I would have to write him a check that would most likely bounce if he beat me to the bank.

"No way." He held up a hand and shook his head, a pained expression on his face.

"Please. You didn't have to do that."

"I know. And I told you, I wanted to. Look, think of it as a … a birthday gift."

"It's not my birthday. Or Ember's."

"Okay, but Ember's just passed, and I missed yours too … I'm assuming. So, they're actually late birthday gifts." He placed his hand on his chest and pasted a pitiful expression on his face. "I'm so sorry that I'm getting your gifts to you so late. I am a terrible friend. But I'll do better next year. I promise."

A small laugh escaped my lips before I had the chance to stop it. "What am I going to do with you?" I shook my head and brought my drink to my lips.

"Hopefully you'll keep me," he said in a soft voice.

My stomach flipped and my pulse quickened, and I silently thanked the owners of Top Shelf for the crappy lighting that hid my blushing cheeks. I took a long drink of the salty martini in my hand, hoping to buy time while I wracked my brain trying to find something clever to say.

A woman's shriek suddenly ripped through the air, and the friendly chatter came to a screeching halt. Heads jerked from one direction to another as the crowded bar searched for the source of the scream.

"Help!" She cried out again.

I craned my neck to see what was going on and spotted the blonde that had been following Brock around most of the night. Her eyes were wild and red-rimmed, and the cheeks just below them were stained with black mascara streaks.

Her head whipped from one side of the bar to the other and after a beat, she stomped her foot. "Help! Someone help!"

"What's wrong?" A man's voice finally called out.

"It's Brock. He's … I think he's dead!"

CHAPTER FOUR

A collective gasp rippled around the room, and she melted into a puddle of heavy sobs on the floor. People began scurrying about in various directions, but I wasn't sure any of them had an actual plan.

I pulled my cell phone from my purse and found my brother's name in my contact list. He answered after the first ring.

I pressed a finger against my free ear to drowned out the surrounding noise. "Matt, you need to get downtown. Now."

"Why?" He sounded groggy, and I knew I'd woken him from a dead sleep.

"Some woman is claiming that Brock Garrett is dead, and I don't know exactly what's going on, but it's devolving into mayhem at this point. We're at Top Shelf," I yelled above the increasing hysteria.

"On my way," he said, though I could barely hear him.

Roman had moved toward the entrance of the bar while I was on the phone with Matt, but he was already making his way back to me with Kiki close behind.

"What's going on?" I asked.

"A few guys are walking over to Brock's place. That's where she says he is. But I need to follow them. If he's alive, we want to save him, but if he's not, they can't be contaminating the crime scene. I just want to make sure they don't."

"Absolutely. Let's go." I set my drink down on the counter and adjusted my purse strap.

"You're going?" Kiki looked surprised.

"Of course I'm going. I'm not going to stay here."

"Uh …" Roman looked like he wanted to protest, but I wasn't going to give him the opportunity. "Kiki, Matt's on his way. Can you call and tell him to come to Brock's place instead of the bar?" I didn't wait for her to respond before I grabbed Roman by the hand and pulled him toward the door.

BROCK GARRETT'S HOUSE WAS ONLY A BLOCK AWAY FROM TOP Shelf and I'd opted to remove my heels so I could keep up with Roman as we hurried down the sidewalk to catch up with the group that had already headed there.

"Ross!" Roman bellowed as soon as we saw the handful of men stationed outside of Brock's door.

A man I didn't recognize was banging on the door with his fist, but they all turned at the sound Roman's voice.

He leaned over to me and said in a low voice, "My voice carries well."

"Obviously." I agreed.

Ross Burkman walked down the concrete path from Brock's front door and met Roman and I just as we started up the walkway. I noticed an expensive looking red sportscar in the driveway with the windshield bashed in and the tires slit.

"The front door is locked. Should we go around and see if the back is open?" Ross asked.

"Why don't you look inside the windows and I'll check the back door?"

Ross sized Roman up and quickly nodded his head in agreement.

I was still barefoot, and the grass was a much welcome relief from the concrete I'd been walking on. I followed Roman around to the back of Brock's house and peered in the windows as we went. Most of the blinds were closed and I couldn't hear any noise coming from inside.

"What's going on over there?" a squeaky voice shouted. I scanned the darkness to see where it was coming from, but all I could see were hedges and a few flower bushes.

"Yoohoo! Over here!" The voice called out again and a porch light sprang to life in front of the house next door. Moira Meeks was standing on her tiptoes and peering over the top of her glasses.

"There's an emergency," I called back to her.

"It's locked." Roman said, moving away from the back door to look inside the nearest window.

"What's the emergency?" Moira yelled.

"Brock. Did you see him come home?" I called back.

She shook her head and hobbled down the steps of her porch.

"Are we even sure that woman knew what she was talking about?" I asked Roman, though I moved to the opposite side of the house to look for a window that might be open.

"No, we aren't." Ross was suddenly at my side.

"So this might be a wild goose chase," I muttered.

Ross was on his phone, but he spoke to me. "He's not answering his cell, though, and we've been banging on the door."

"Maybe he isn't even here." I moved in front of a long

window where I saw a sliver of light and pressed my forehead up against the glass. A light shone from a room across the hall and at first, it appeared empty. An unmade bed of silky sheets and a comforter, a lamp with a red shade to give it a sexy vibe, but no Brock. Except there was a Brock and I'd only missed him because he was fixed to the ceiling. I blinked a few times in rapid succession and held my breath, pressing my forehead harder against the window. A man's body — Brock's body — was secured to the ceiling somehow, his arms dangling limply toward the floor, and blood dripped in a rhythmic stream.

"Roman." My voice was hoarse, and it came out as a whisper. I peeled my eyes away from the window and tried again. "Roman!" This time, I was sure the whole neighborhood heard me, because about a dozen people surrounded me in a matter of seconds. The sound of sirens growing closer only brought the reality home. Brock Garrett was definitely dead.

CHAPTER FIVE

If you think word spreads fast in a small town, you should see how fast it spreads in a small town full of folks with magic. The crowd in front of Brock's house spread back so far that I couldn't even see where it ended. The police were doing their best to contain the gawkers and move everyone along, but they weren't very successful.

I stood in the middle of Brock's front yard with Roman on one side and Moira Meeks on the other. I clutched one three-inch pump in either hand and waited impatiently for my brother to exit Brock's house.

I shivered despite the warmth of the island night.

"I'm sorry. I don't have a jacket to offer you." Roman placed an arm around my shoulders and rubbed my arms with his hands to warm me up.

"It's just from the adrenaline," I said, fighting back the urge to let my teeth chatter.

I could feel Moira's eyes on me, and I avoided looking in her direction. I wasn't in the mood for her attitude.

"Did you see the car in the driveway?" I asked Roman.

"Yeah, Moira, did you hear anything? I'd think smashing a windshield would make quite a bit of noise."

She screwed up her face like she was thinking. "No, I didn't hear anything tonight, but I'm a little confused. See, someone messed his car all up about a week ago, but he'd had it fixed. I saw him pulling in the driveway just yesterday and it was as good as new."

"So, someone destroyed his car for a second time in a week?"

"Looks that way," she said, peering around me to peek at the car.

"That is my niece right there and I swear on every deity in the history of deities, if you don't get the hell out of my way, I will curse you seven ways to Sunday!" I instantly breathed a sigh of relief at the sound of Aunt Hattie bellowing threats at a very frightened-looking police officer.

He was at least a foot and a half taller than her, but she had taken on an aggressive stance as she waved one hand in the air.

"I've got it." Roman gave me a quick wink before he went to save the police officer from Aunt Hattie's wrath. I watched him speak in a hushed voice to the cop, and after a few moments, he stepped aside to allow Aunt Hattie to pass. She glared at the officer over her shoulder and I swore I saw her muttering under her breath. I waited until she was close before I asked the inevitable question.

"So, what kind of curse did you put on him?"

She looked around me at Moira Meeks and must've decided she was in good company because she finally said, "Ah, nothing big. His wand is just going to sprout flowers instead of magic every time he uses it for the next twenty-four hours."

I smirked. "Aunt Hattie, what if he needs it for something serious?"

She shrugged. "Not really my problem. It's a harmless curse, Shay. Don't get all Mary Sue on me."

"Aunt Hattie?" Matt had a surprised look on his face as he approached. "How did you get past the … oh, never mind." He mumbled and ran a hand through his hair. "How are you feeling, Shay?"

"Fine." I shivered again. "Really."

"Do you know what happened yet?" Roman stood behind me and placed his hands on my arms, speaking to Matt over the top of my head.

"Not the specifics, of course, but there's enough evidence to come to some obvious conclusions."

"Like?" Aunt Hattie asked.

"I'm getting to it," he said in a terse tone. "The blood you saw dripping wasn't from a typical wound that could be made by a weapon. Brock was bitten."

"Bitten?" I felt the hair on my arms raise. "Are you saying …"

"Yeah. Vampire bite." He nodded and worked his jaw for a full beat before he continued. "Not the type to turn him either. The type to kill him. This was definitely a murder."

The memory of Brock lying flush against the ceiling invaded my mind. "How was he on the ceiling like that?"

"We think it must've been some kind of enchantment. At present, we aren't really sure what the point of it was other than perhaps a strange game the killer was playing."

I shuddered, and this time it wasn't from the effects of adrenaline.

"We haven't had a vampire attack around here in …" Aunt Hattie looked up and her eyes darted back and forth as she tried to recall the information. "Gosh, I can't even remember. I was in my early thirties, I think."

"I'm not sure this was a vampire attack so much as it was a murder that just so happened to be committed by a vampire," Matt said.

"Well, do you believe me now?" Moira Meeks cocked her head to the side and looked up at Matt.

"I beg your pardon?" He knit his brow and rested his hands on his duty belt.

Moira let out a frustrated groan and threw her hands in the air. "About the stalker! I've been telling you someone's been stalking me, and now my neighbor is dead. That can't be a coincidence. He must've caught them or something, and they killed him to conceal their identity."

Matt scratched at the scruff on his chin while he contemplated what she'd said. "I think you might be onto something, ma'am. Would you come down to the station and we can talk there?"

"Finally! It takes a man being killed for you to do something. Ridiculous!" She spun around and marched across the yard toward her house.

"Is that a yes?" Matt called out after her.

She waved her hand in the air but didn't look back.

"You really think Brock saw her stalker and they killed him?" Roman asked.

"Brock had enough enemies of his own," I replied.

"Vampire enemies, in fact." Roman added.

"That's what I've been hearing. He had a big fight with Lara Gratz this evening." Matt let his gaze linger on me for a moment while he worked his jaw.

"Matt, you can't possibly think she did this," I said, a bit taken aback.

"I didn't say that. Why don't you tell me what you saw tonight?"

"Yeah, she had an argument with him, but then she left with Gretchen. He also had an argument with Roman—"

"Roman isn't a vampire." Matt cut in.

"Okay, well, it doesn't sound like Ross Burkman's business partner cared for him much. Craig something."

"Baldwin," Roman said.

"Yeah, Craig Baldwin. Honestly, Matt, I saw Brock have tense interactions with multiple people this evening, and a lot of them were vampires."

"But only one of them threatened to kill him." he said with a hint of smugness.

"Are you even one-hundred percent sure it's a vampire bite?" Aunt Hattie asked.

"What do you mean? It's hard to mistake." He scrunched up his face.

"Maybe it was only made to look like one. Maybe they used some kind of object."

"Oh, that's a great theory!" I said a little too eagerly.

Aunt Hattie raised her chin in triumph and grinned at Matt.

"It's a theory that we'll be exploring. Listen"—he paused to give us each a pointed look— "You two need to get home and let us do the investigating. I don't want you trying to get involved. Roman, can you please make sure my great aunt and sister make it home safely?"

"Of course." Roman squeezed my arms.

"We're not getting involved, Matt." I stood firmly in place. "I'm a witness, and you basically accused one of our oldest family friends of murder. I'm already involved whether you like it or not."

"Shay," he said in that same warning tone that my father always did. "You know what I mean. You've already given your statement and there's nothing more you can do here tonight. Go home. Check on your daughter."

"Whoa. My daughter is at her friend's house for the night. And I don't like the tone you're taking with me."

"Yeah, you think you're mister big stuff just because you have that uniform on." Aunt Hattie squared her shoulders. "I could end you right here right now."

"Calm down, Aunt Hattie." I put a hand on her arm and pulled her back.

"You need to go home, ladies." Matt turned and walked away, leaving us standing in the middle of Brock's front yard.

Aunt Hattie started to mumble under her breath again, but I interrupted her.

"That's enough cursing for tonight, you." I grabbed Roman's arm to steady myself and put my shoes back on.

"I don't like his attitude sometimes," Aunt Hattie grumbled. "Makes a person wonder who raised him."

"You raised him." I laughed and Roman was doing his best to hide the smile on his face.

"Nope, not me. I'm not taking credit for that one. Kiki neither."

"What did Kiki do?" I snickered.

Aunt Hattie threw her head back and let out a melodramatic sigh.

"All right. Sorry I asked." I slung my arm around her. "Does that mean you're taking credit for me?"

"Yes. You're my favorite."

"I knew it!" I said, much louder than I intended to.

"Knew what? What's going on?" I saw Lara standing just behind the crime scene tape. Her face was so etched with worry that I nearly didn't recognize her.

"Oh, no. Nothing about … this." I motioned to the house behind me.

"What's happened? This guy won't tell me anything." She narrowed her eyes at the police officer whom Aunt Hattie had cursed earlier.

I drew closer so the surrounding crowd couldn't hear me. "You don't know?"

She shook her head. "All I know is that people are saying he's dead. Is he?"

Her eyes searched mine with an intensity that forced me to break eye contact for a moment.

"He is … Lara, where did you go when you left the bar?"

She furrowed her brow and cast a sidelong glance at the officer standing nearby. "I took a walk to cool off. Why?"

I really wasn't sure how much I should tell her. Not because I thought she was guilty, but I was afraid that she'd waste her genuine surprise on me instead of the police, who needed to see her true reaction. I knew how much they read into those things. My mind raced with possible scenarios, but fortunately, I didn't have to make a decision either way.

"Lara Gratz?" I recognized the voice of the Chief of Police as soon I heard it. It wasn't particularly grating in and of itself, but the person that it was attached to made it sound like nails on a chalkboard.

"Chief." The police officer acknowledged the Chief of Police without looking down at him. Huh. Maybe Moira Meeks was right—maybe some short people found it offensive.

"I'm Lara." She wrapped her arms around herself as Gretchen and Mina pushed to the front of the crowd.

"I'd like you to come with me, ma'am," Chief Leach said.

"What for?" Gretchen huffed, finally coming up beside her sister.

"We need to speak with her."

"Yes, obviously. But why?" Gretchen pushed a handful of red curls back from her face.

Chief Leach placed his hands on his hips and looked back and forth between Lara and Gretchen. "It's a private matter. We'll actually be interested in speaking with you, too."

"It's probably because you two saw him in the bar tonight. I wouldn't worry." Mina tried to sound reassuring, but her voice wavered.

"Lara, you didn't do anything wrong. You have nothing to worry about," Gretchen added.

"All right then. Let's go." Chief Leach held up the tape and allowed Lara to pass under.

Gretchen attempted to duck down under it as well, but he dropped it, nearly smacking her in the face. "Just her. I'll send someone over to talk with you later."

"But I was there, too! The same time as Lara!" Gretchen called out after him.

Chief Leach didn't look back as he led Lara along Brock's front lawn to a police cruiser. After she was inside, he closed the door and moved away, and she met my gaze, the worry in her eyes growing deeper. I wasn't sure what to do as both of her sisters struggled not to burst into tears.

"It'll be okay. She's just being questioned, that's all."

"What if it's not?" Mina asked. "What if they really think she did it?"

"She can't go down for this." Gretchen said resolutely. "She just can't."

I tore my eyes away from Lara's and looked at the fear on her sisters' faces. "Then she won't. I'll make sure of it."

CHAPTER SIX

"Shay, I told you I can't talk about this with you." I followed Matt around the kitchen counter, ignoring his blatant attempt to get away from me.

"Can you at least tell me if it was for sure a vampire? Do you know yet?"

He let out a prolonged sigh and set his cup of coffee down. He rolled his neck from one side to the other and glanced at Paige, who was arranging tiny plastic body parts on the counter. "Honey, why are you disassembling people in the kitchen?"

"I'm not. I'm *assembling* them. I'm making Shay and Ember." she said without looking up. "Shay, would you prefer something casual or a bit fancier? Saturday errands or date night?"

"Well, seeing as how I don't know what I would even wear on a date—"

"You'd better!" Her head snapped up and she wore a serious expression on her face. "Roman is bound to ask you. And soon. You need to be prepared."

I felt my cheeks flush. "He is not. I wish everyone would stop saying stuff like that. We're just friends."

"Nu-uh. Matt and Roman are friends. You and Roman are ..." She looked at Matt for help and he held his hands up in surrender.

"I'm staying out of this one."

"Good. You should. You all should." I gave Paige a pointed look. "Besides, we have more pressing issues to discuss. Right, Matt?"

"You know, you might drive me crazy. Literally, actually crazy." He smirked and shook his head.

"And what kind of sister would I be if I didn't?" I smiled sweetly. "Now, back to the topic at hand. Was it a vampire bite?"

"It certainly appears so," he answered curtly.

"Okay! This is good. We're making progress. Right, Paige?"

She was engrossed in studying a small square of pink fabric. "I don't think pink works. It's not really your color." She set the fabric down and began sifting through a large storage container filled with various types and colors of fabric.

"No, it's definitely not." I waved a hand dismissively and turned my attention back to Matt. "Anyway, what about Lara? Has she been arrested? You seemed pretty adamant that she was a suspect, and I watched Chief Leach take her away the other night."

"She wasn't arrested, though. Just questioned." He stared down into his coffee cup.

"And? Was she cleared?"

The sound of raucous laughter crackled through the air just above the thundering of small feet coming down the hall. My ten-year-old niece, Fallon, came around the corner first, a hand-held gaming device in her hand.

"Aunt Shay!" She beamed and ran over to give me a hug.

"Aunt Shay!" My eight-year-old nephew, MJ, followed suit. He was the spitting image of my brother and seeing him often felt like I'd just stepped out of a time machine.

"Hey, buddy." I squeezed him close. "What are you playing?"

"Gods and Goddesses." Fallon answered for him.

"Hmm ... I don't think I've heard of that one."

"It's fun. I'll show you how to play," MJ said.

"That sounds great, but maybe next time, okay? I have some errands that I need to get to. I just stopped by to talk to your dad for a minute." I ruffled his mop of sandy blond hair and looked back to my brother.

"So? Cleared?"

"Fallon, put that back and get out of my supply bin," Paige scolded.

I snickered and made a funny face at Fallon. "Paige, you realize you're telling a little girl she can't play with your dolls, right?"

"They're not dolls, Shay. They're miniatures," she scoffed and attempted to shoo both children away.

"All right, guys, come on. Out of mom's hair," Matt said, motioning them out of the kitchen.

"Matt?" I pleaded.

"I can't discuss this with you, Shay. Please stop asking."

"I just want to help."

"You can help by staying out of it," he said in a stern tone that caused even Paige to finally look up from her project.

"Matt, you don't need to talk to her like that." She pursed her lips.

"Fine. You two have a nice day." He threw up his hand and waved over his shoulder as he headed for the front door. I waited for Fallon and MJ to run out to the backyard before I spoke.

"Sorry for making him grumpy this morning," I offered.

"No, it's not you. He's grumpy every time he has a murder investigation. He's even grumpier because of the whole vampire thing and Lara Gratz." She was already back to holding up different colored fabrics to the Shay doll.

"Have you seen anything? Anything at all?" I asked. Paige had visions sometimes, and even though they were usually only snapshots, they always proved to be accurate.

She shook her head and placed a strip of black fabric over the doll. "I wish I had. It would be nice to help lead the police in the right direction, but I haven't had one related to the murder yet."

"That's it." I motioned to the black fabric that still lay over the doll. "Black. It's my signature color."

She giggled and set to work pulling her sewing machine from the large case on the floor. "I did, however, have a vision about you."

"Oh?" I tried to act nonchalant, but I wasn't very good at it. It wasn't a Graves family strength.

Paige gave me a coy smile. "Remember when I told you that you should be prepared for a date?"

I felt my stomach flip and I pretended to be interested in one of the dolls on the table in front of me. "Yeah, kind of."

"Well, that was my vision. You were going on a date."

"What was the vision *exactly* though? I want the details."

"Well," she began to cut strips of the shiny black fabric with a pair of shears. "I saw you standing inside of Brews Brothers and you were talking to someone — I couldn't see exactly who, but I think we all know — and you said 'yes, I'd love to be your date. I'll meet you there at seven.' Then the vision faded."

"Huh."

"So, like I said, be prepared." She glanced up at me over the top of her sewing machine with a wide grin.

"Stop it," I said, fidgeting uncomfortably with a string that had fallen from the fabric Paige was cutting.

Something about Paige's vision didn't seem right. At least, not if Roman was the man I was supposed to go out with. I was comfortable enough with him that I would've let him pick me up at home. Though maybe there were other circumstances I just wasn't aware of yet. Either way, Paige's visions were never wrong, which meant I did, in fact, need to prepare myself for a date.

CHAPTER SEVEN

*D*espite Paige's prediction—or, warning, rather—I needed to see Roman. He was the only person that could help me work through the details of the murder. I knew Ember would be home from her friend Chloe's house around noon, so that gave me exactly three hours. He always spent his Saturday mornings at the Tribune, so after shooting him a quick text, I hopped in my car and headed in his direction.

I ventured off Shadow Lane and onto Wolfsbane toward town. The sign for Lettuce Inn came into view and I made a snap decision, yanking on the steering wheel of my car and nearly careening off the road and into the ditch. I didn't have my wand out, but I was able to pull my magic from within. The car came to a halt, the front bumper hovering above the ditch, and then slowly glided backwards until it was safely on the road. My hands were shaking when I finally let the car roll up the front drive in front of the old renovated house. Gretchen and Lara sat on the front porch, rocking aimlessly on the porch swing.

"Nice save." Gretchen called out.

"Yeah, thanks. It was close," I huffed as I climbed the steps up to large wraparound porch.

"I hope I'm not interrupting."

"Not at all, dear." Gretchen gave me a welcoming smile.

"I just wanted to check on you," I said, leaning against the porch railing. I realized my hands were still shaking from my near-death and I shoved them in my pockets. "Are you all doing okay?"

They glanced at each other, but Lara was the one to speak. "Honestly, Shay, I'm not doing great. The police seem to be really focused on me."

"Your brother, to be exact." Gretchen said wryly.

I shifted uncomfortably, suddenly unsure what to do with my feet. I pulled my hands from my pockets and crossed my arms over my chest. It was strange; the Gratz sisters looked only a few years older than me, but they'd turned long before I was born so I'd grown up knowing them as adults. In spite of the fact that they weren't technically my elders anymore, my inner child still saw them that way.

"Listen, I have no control over what Matt does, but I'm trying very hard to convince anyone that will listen that you didn't have anything to do with Brock's murder."

"How do you know she didn't though?" Gretchen asked.

I drew back, surprised by her question. "Because I know Lara. I've known her all my life."

Gretchen eyed me for a moment longer than was comfortable before she gave me a slight nod.

"Don't be hard on her, Gretch. None of this is her fault." Lara patted her sister's leg. "Thank you for believing in me, Shay. It seems you're one of the few people in this town that does."

Tears rimmed Lara's eyes and she wiped at them with the sleeve of her sweater.

"Aren't you roasting?" I asked. No matter the season, Mystic Key always had the perfect summer weather. Coming from the cold, rainy Pacific Northwest, I was still adjusting to the heat and found myself blotting at my sweaty forehead more often than seemed appropriate.

The screen door flew open, and Mina appeared holding a tray with three glasses. "Vampires don't feel the heat, Shay." She placed the tray down on the table in front of the porch swing. "Sorry, I didn't know you were out here. Want something to drink? We've got …" She tapped her chin with her finger. "Well, we've got water. I can make some coffee—"

"No, no. It's fine. I'm not staying. I just wanted to check on Lara." I watched as Gretchen reached for the tall silver pitcher and poured a dark red liquid into each glass.

"That's blood, isn't it?" I blurted out.

Gretchen smirked and handed a glass to each of her sisters. "It's funny, no matter how long someone has lived in Mystic Key, they still get uncomfortable when the vamps drink blood."

"It's synthetic anyway." Mina plopped down next to Gretchen on the swing. "It only looks real."

"Except for the golden stuff," Lara said.

"Golden stuff?" I asked.

"You haven't heard of it?" Mina widened her eyes in disbelief.

"Most people haven't." Lara wiped a bit of red liquid from her upper lip. "It's not exactly common, even among our type."

"Can someone tell me what golden blood is?" I asked, glancing down at my watch. I wanted to be sure I caught Roman before he left his office, but I was also intrigued by the golden blood concept.

"I can do you one better. I can show you." Mina jumped up and hurried into the Inn.

Gretchen took a long drink from her glass and set it back down on the tray in front of her. "Basically, the way it works is this. The store in town, B Positive, sells eight main types of synthetic blood. That's your A positive, O negative, etcetera. It's further divided down by other factors, but let's keep this simple. All blood is flavored differently, and we each have our preferences. It's like preferring orange juice to apple, right?"

I nodded along, thoroughly intrigued by the lesson.

"So, the most common is the cheapest and it goes up in price from there. O positive is the most common so it's the lowest priced. AB negative is one of the rarest. The difference between the two is like buying an eight-dollar bottle of wine versus a fifty-dollar bottle. You following?"

"Yup."

"Okay, golden blood is the rarest possible. Only forty-three people in the world have been reported to have it. As such, the price for it—even its synthetic version because all synthetic blood still has to take its flavor profile from real blood—is astronomical. We're talking only the richest of the rich can afford this stuff."

Mina appeared in the doorway again, a purple jug in her hands. She took timid steps toward me, her eyes fixed on the vessel in her hands. She stopped just inches in front of me and carefully removed the lid.

"Don't breathe on it," she whispered.

I leaned over and stared down at the contents and sucked in a quick breath. Inside, thick gold liquid glittered and swirled as if it were alive.

"Breathtaking, isn't it." Gretchen didn't ask, but rather stated.

I nodded, still holding my breath, and took a few steps back. Once I was safely away, I exhaled. "It's gorgeous."

Mina replaced the lid and turned to take it back inside.

"I can see why it's so expensive." I mused. "I don't mean to be rude here, but how is it that you all have it?"

"It's a fair question." Lara snorted out a laugh. "We have a guest that drinks it."

"You do?" I didn't mean to sound as shocked as I was, but Mystic Key was littered with some of the most fabulous resorts in the world. I was struggling to understand why someone that rich would choose to stay at the Lettuce Inn instead.

"She was at the resort, but people found out who she was and they kept bothering her so she moved here."

"Who is it?" I asked.

Gretchen and Lara looked at each other for a brief moment like they were communicating telepathically.

"You promise not to tell anyone?" Lara asked in a hushed voice.

"We mean *anyone*." Gretchen said firmly.

"Yeah, of course."

"It's Arabel Onassis." Lara widened her eyes like she was anticipating my reaction.

I wracked my brain trying to recall the name, but I was coming up empty. "Is that an actress?"

The sisters glanced at each other again before looking back at me in disbelief. "You seriously don't know who she is?"

"Should I?" I suddenly felt as uncool as I did when Ember raved about a new band that I'd never heard of.

"You know Rudolph Lebeau at least, right?"

"Yes. I definitely know him." Rudolph Lebeau was a fashion designer who was extremely popular among paranormals and lived and worked in Mystic Key.

"Okay, she's even more famous than him, but she only does limited-edition stuff."

"Because she makes her own fabric too!" Gretchen cut in excitedly.

Lara shushed her before continuing in a quiet voice. "Anyway, she's in town because they did a secret collaboration together, and there's a fashion show to reveal their new line."

"Wow. I'm surprised Kiki didn't mention it. She loves stuff like that."

"She probably doesn't know yet. Like I said, it's a secret and they're only announcing it to the public a couple of days before the event. I guess a lot of fancy schmancy people are flying in for it though. We only know about it because she's staying here."

"She did invite us though, which is neat," Gretchen said.

Lara's eyes were downcast, and she fidgeted with the hem of her sweater. "Hopefully I'm not in jail by then."

"You won't be." Gretchen's expression hardened.

"Lara, I don't mean to pry …"—That wasn't exactly true. I was definitely prying— "But do you have an alibi?"

She drew her lower lip between her teeth and let out a deep breath. "Not really."

"Yes, you do. I'm your alibi. That's what I've told the police too." Gretchen set her mouth in a hard line and by the way Lara was looking at her, I had a feeling she was lying. And that fact wouldn't bode well for either of them.

THE MYSTIC KEY TRIBUNE OFFICE WAS LOCATED RIGHT IN THE middle of town, and I was lucky to snag a parking spot right out front. I had never been inside before, but I was surprised to see that it was humble in both size and decor. Fiona, a reporter with both a bad attitude and a crush on Roman, looked up from her computer when I entered and didn't make any effort to hide the scowl on her face.

I assumed Roman had a private office somewhere, but unless another employee was in, I was going to have to ask Fiona where it was.

I squared my shoulders and lifted my chin, letting my gaze settle on her. She curled her upper lip and gave me a once-over before flipping her blond hair over her shoulder.

"Hiya, Shay!" Relief washed over me as Corbin Grimes seemingly appeared out of nowhere.

I offered Fiona one final glare before smiling at Corbin. "Hey, Corbin. I'm looking for Roman."

"Right this way, madame." He bent slightly at the waist, a huge grin still plastered on his face, and I followed him past Fiona's desk and down the hallway.

Corbin was a fairy and I was mesmerized by the way his iridescent wings sparkled as the light bounced off them. I examined how perfectly his dress shirt was cut to allow his wings to be free. I'd never really paid much attention, but it was quite interesting how clothing was made for paranormals.

"I like your shirt," I said to his back.

"Oh, thank you! It's a Rudolph Lebeau." He looked back at me over his shoulder.

"Does anyone else design clothes for fairies?"

"Yes, but Rudolph's stuff is the most fashion-forward and affordable on the market. And with my salary," he stopped in front of a closed door and rapped lightly before leaning in to whisper, "I need both."

"Come in." The sound of Roman's voice made my heart

beat a little faster. Corbin pushed open the door and stepped aside so I could enter.

I thanked him and waited until he closed the door behind me before I turned my attention to Roman. He sat behind his desk, a friendly smile on his face and a pencil shoved behind his ear.

"Sit, please." He motioned to the chair across the desk from him. "Can I get you anything? Water, tea, coffee?"

"No thanks." I held the back of my dress close to my legs as I lowered myself into a chair that boasted an orange floral pattern straight out of the seventies. Paige's words suddenly entered my mind, and I became a little too self-aware. I tucked my hair behind one ear and then pulled it back over. Twice.

"So," I said, hoping to provoke a conversation that would move his focus from me to something else. "Thanks for letting me come by this morning. I know you're busy, but I was hoping we could hash out some of the details of the Brock Garrett case."

He leaned back in his chair and crossed his arms over his chest, a knowing smile creeping onto his face.

"You have details?" he asked.

"Some. And you have some too."

"I do … I take it Matt wouldn't talk to you?" He cocked an eyebrow.

"Did he talk to you?" I shot the question back at him.

"Answering a question with a question. That's one way to deflect," he teased.

"I'm very good at deflecting. It's one of my strengths."

He snickered and pulled the pencil from over his ear. He sifted through a pile of papers before landing on one filled with chicken scratch.

"All right …" he scanned the paper like he was looking for something specific. "Here we go. So, what I've figured out is that Brock left the bar at roughly ten p.m. Top Shelf has a security camera pointed directly at the sidewalk in front of the entrance."

"Have you seen the tape?"

"Yeah, and I have to be honest. It doesn't look good for Lara." His forehead creased. "She grabbed him around the neck, Shay."

"What?" I nearly shouted.

"Yeah, she took off before he did. I'm sure you remember that. But when he left the bar, she sort of came out of nowhere. She ran up to him and got in his face, he laughed, and she tried to strangle him. After a few seconds, he managed to pull her off. He walked away in the direction of his house. She stood outside and had a cigarette, and once she was done, she went in the same direction."

"Oh, crap." A knot formed in the pit of my stomach.

"My sentiments exactly." He tapped the eraser end of the pencil against the stack of papers in front of him. "*But ...* that still doesn't make her guilty."

"No, it doesn't. How were you able to see the tape, anyway?"

He gave me a lopsided grin. "I know the bartender pretty well."

"Do you know all the bartenders in this town?" I teased. It was thanks to Roman's friendship with the bartender of Bar Humbug that we found pertinent information about two murders only a couple of months before.

He shrugged. "It's important to have the right connections. It just so happens that bartenders have a lot of good intel."

"I'll bet. So, what about what happens before and after Brock leaves and Lara follows? Anyone else go in the direction of his house?"

He scratched at his beard and made a disappointed face. "Only Morty Mortenson, but he was back before Brock left. As for what happened after, well, that's where we have a problem. Something obstructed the camera."

"What do you mean?"

"Not sure what it was, but something covered it. The bartender said there's a light that attracts bugs at night, so most likely one of them rested on the camera lens and stayed there for a while. Either way, we don't have any footage of the two hours immediately after Lara walked out of view."

"Well that's just great." I said. I thought about the events of the night Brock died and ran through a list of possible suspects in my mind. A face suddenly sprang to the forefront. "Remember Craig Baldwin?" I asked.

Roman looked thoughtful for a moment before recognition dawned on his face. "Yeah, he was the tan vampire, right? Partners with the wolf shifter leader?"

"That's him. He made no bones about the fact that he had a deep hatred for Brock. I also didn't see him after Brock left the bar."

Roman began scribbling on the paper.

"There was also the woman he was talking to that night. I don't know her name, but she was the one who came screaming into the bar that he was dead."

He continued to scribble as he spoke. "Kara Brewer. And boy, is she a real piece of work." He stopped writing and began sifting through the papers again. "Turns out she'd been having a fling with Brock off and on over the past few months. She really thought he was going to settle down with her, and when she caught him with another woman at his place, she completely lost it. Smashed the windows in his car and everything. He forgave her eventually which, wow," he said with widened eyes, "but then she devised a plan to get pregnant because she thought he'd be forced to marry her."

"For shifter's sake." I muttered.

"Right? Anyway, he figured it out and cut ties with her again. I guess the night he died was the first time he'd seen her since. Her story was that after he left, she decided to go to his house to try to talk with him or ... something."

"And she found him dead?"

"That's what she says. I guess she saw him in the window just like you did."

"Hmm ... so he probably didn't answer the door, and she proceeded to creep around outside looking in the windows," I said.

"That's what I'm thinking. If, of course, she's telling the truth."

"Right. What's with the vampire-like bite marks though? Do you think it really was a vampire?"

"That's what's confusing me." He furrowed his brow and studied his notes again. "They are indicative of a vampire attack and they did find venom. But it doesn't look like the body was missing any blood aside from the small amount from the wounds."

"So, it wasn't a vampire-driven murder, but a murder committed by a vampire. Which is what Matt already suspected," I said.

He nodded and leaned back in his chair again. "Brock had a lot of enemies. Woman that he'd scorned, people he'd tried browbeating into selling him their property for his stupid gym. And, just all around being a jerk. I think it's going to be harder to nail down a suspect pool because so many people have a decent motive."

"True. I mean, you could even argue Aunt Hattie did."

"What do you mean?"

"Oh, I guess he came by the funeral home and Aunt Hattie happened to be the one he spoke to. She said he was terrible, and she sent him on his way."

Roman suddenly pushed back from his desk and jumped to his feet. "Let's go talk to her."

"What? Now?"

"Maybe he said something to her that can help."

"Maybe." I rose, skeptical that Aunt Hattie had let Brock stick around long enough to reveal anything of value. "She's at home, I think."

"Great. I'll meet you there."

CHAPTER EIGHT

*R*oman followed me to Shadow Lane, and we both parked in my driveway and walked over to Aunt Hattie's house. The front door was open, and I could hear her yelling at Tito before we'd even made it up the front steps.

"I can't believe you're going to ruin this for me!" she hollered.

I glanced and Roman and offered little more than a shrug before I led the way into the house.

Tito, Aunt Hattie's miniature dragon, was perched on top of a tall bookshelf. Aunt Hattie stood below, jabbing her wand up into the air and shooting spurts of magic at him. Tito was fast though, and he was able to dodge them like something out of the Matrix.

"Aunt Hattie, why are you trying to kill your familiar?" I asked.

"I'm not trying to kill him," she said without taking her eyes off of him. "I'm trying to force him to do my will."

"Ah, even better." I plopped down on the couch and took in the scene, motioning for Roman to sit next to me. He sat down close enough that his leg rested against mine. "So, what is it you want him to do, anyway?" I asked her.

"I have an event today and he doesn't want to come." She flicked her wand and Tito dove to the left, sending a small skeleton figurine crashing to the floor.

"Now look what you've done! You broke Mr. Bones." She hissed.

"So? Just go without him," I said.

She stopped and turned slowly until I could see the scowl on her face. "How am I supposed to be an accurate representation of a pirate without a parrot?"

"Um … I don't mean to interrupt, but I feel like I'm missing some important information." Roman looked over at me.

"You've heard of LARPing, right? Live action role play? Aunt Hattie does a pirate-themed one. She makes Tito play the parrot on her shoulder."

He blinked slowly, utter confusion etched on his perfect features.

"I know. It's a waste of time to try to make rational sense of anything around here. You just gotta go with it." I looked up at Tito, still cowering on the top of the bookshelf. "Why won't you go with her today?"

"Because I don't enjoy it, Shay. I have better things to do with my time."

"He demanded I compensate him," Aunt Hattie said, appalled.

"Yes, I did." Tito ventured to rise back up.

"That's ludicrous!" she shouted.

"Pay me!" he shouted back.

She pointed her wand up at him again and he breathed the smallest puff of fire out at her.

My cell phone buzzed in my pocket and I pulled it out to see a text from Ember.

Ember: Where are you? I see your car in the driveway.

Me: Over at Aunt Hattie's. I'll be back soon.

Ember: OK. Going to make cookies.

Me: Don't burn down the house.

I shoved my phone back in my pocket and raised my voice so I could be heard over the ruckus. "All right, you two. Can you pause this for a moment? We need to talk to you, Aunt Hattie."

She gave one final jab of her wand up at Tito before she wandered over to sit on the couch across from us. She lowered herself slowly and leaned back, an angry scowl fixed on her face.

"What do you want?" she asked, still glaring daggers at her familiar.

"You remember how you told me Brock Garrett came by recently to ask about the funeral business?"

She scrunched up her face and looked heavenward.

"Wolf shifter. Kind of a jerk," I prompted.

"Oh!" She slapped her leg. "Yes, I do remember." A devilish grin spread across her face.

"What did you do?" I asked.

"I told him to go away, but he was persistent. Forceful almost. I rewarded him by offering a cup of special tea."

"*And*? What did you do to it?" I asked.

She shrugged but smiled gleefully. "He seemed to think he was pretty hot stuff, you know? The kind of guy that thinks he's far more charming and handsome than he actually is." She stuck her finger up to her mouth and made a fake gagging motion. "I've always hated men like that."

"So … what did you do?" I pressed.

Her eyes darted back forth between Roman and me, and she giggled like a schoolgirl. "No woman likes a fella that smells like dirty old gym socks."

I snorted and shook my head at the second immature curse she'd come up with in the last twenty-four hours. "Okay, Aunt Hattie, can you tell us about your conversation with him?"

She shrugged and spoke in a mild tone. "There's not much to tell, really. He was asking about buying some of the grave-yard property. I told him to get lost. He wouldn't shut up. Kept trying to sell me on the idea. So, I faked the sweet old lady routine and offered him some tea. I let him yammer on until I was sure he'd drank enough of it, and then I kicked him out."

"Did he give any indication about where he was going, where he'd just come from, anything like that?" I asked.

"Why?" Tito dove from the bookshelf and landed on the back of the couch just behind Aunt Hattie's shoulder.

"Because we're trying to figure out who killed him," Roman answered.

"I wish I could help, but I wasn't paying much attention to him. He was like the teacher talking on Charlie Brown."

Tito laughed at Aunt Hattie's joke and she reached her hand up to give him a gentle pat on the head. Guess the feud was over … temporarily.

"What's Matt got to say?" she asked.

"Matt won't talk to me about the case."

She cocked an eyebrow and I knew she'd caught the bite of bitterness in my tone. Fortunately, she didn't comment on it. "And why are the two of you looking into it?"

"Because the police think Lara Gratz did it and I don't buy it. I just want to help her," I said.

"Lara? Nah, she's the nicest one of those three. Now,

Gretchen, that one's got a temper." Aunt Hattie wagged her finger.

"You know, Gretchen *was* there that night too," I said, my mind racing with possibilities. "But ... I still don't know. We've known the Gratz sisters for a long time, and I just can't see any of them killing someone."

A sudden commotion came from the front of the house in the form of loud thuds and something crashing to the floor. I jumped to my feet and whipped around to see my cat, Steve, zooming toward us. "Shay, come quick! It's an emergency!" He turned just as quickly and headed back the way he'd come.

"Wait! Where? What's going on?"

"At home! It's Ember!" he yelled back over his shoulder.

CHAPTER NINE

My heart pounded so hard I could feel it in my throat. Dread sat in my stomach like a stone, weighing me down as I raced up the front steps to my house. I heard footsteps behind me, and I knew Roman and Aunt Hattie were close.

Steve had already gone inside, evident by the cat door still swinging back and forth.

I grasped the door handle and yanked it open with so much force that it swung back and hit me hard from behind, sending me down onto my hands and knees against the floor. I tried to scramble to my feet, wobbly and unsteady — much like a newborn baby deer — and Roman's strong grip at my waist helped me finally find my footing. I didn't see Ember anywhere, and I was just about to make a beeline for the stairs when Steve's voice called out to me.

"Kitchen!"

I sprinted toward the sound of Steve's voice and rounded the corner just in time to see Ember on the floor. Her back was pressed against the cupboards and her knees were pulled to her chest. Her arms wrapped around them so tightly that I could see the blanched skin on her shins. The look on her face was nothing short of terror as she stared up at the ghostly man in front of her.

He had his back to me but given the too-tight shirt and trendy haircut, I knew exactly who it was.

"Brock," I took a few timid steps in his direction. It was possible he was confused and didn't understand he was dead quite yet, so I didn't want to do anything to upset him. He spun around and I was surprised to see a big, goofy grin on his face.

"I remember you!" He waved but his face fell almost instantly. "I remember you, too," he said over the top of my head and I knew Roman must have been standing behind me.

"How did you get here?" I asked.

He motioned to Ember still sitting on the floor. "She brought me."

"What do you mean?" I asked, brushing past him. I crouched down next to her and ran my hand over the top of her head, smoothing her hair. "Are you okay?" I asked her.

Her eyes searched mine and I could tell she was in shock. "I was making cookies."

"Yes, I know, sweetie." I put my arm around her and glanced up to see a mixing bowl and a handful of ingredients sprawled out on the kitchen counter.

"She used her wand, Shay." Steve sauntered over and plopped down on his haunches.

"Tattle tale," Ember hissed.

"Oh, boy." I sighed and pulled back to look at her.

"I thought I could ..." she sniffed and shook her head, examining the wand on the floor next to her. "I don't know what I was thinking."

"She summoned me," Brock said.

"Yeah, I got that part," I snapped.

"You know you're dead then?" Aunt Hattie was never one to mince words.

A grave look clouded his features. "Yup. Figured that one out pretty quick."

"Do you know who killed you?" Roman asked.

He searched the ceiling for a few moments before casting his eyes down to the floor. "My memory is really foggy. I remember some things, but no, I don't know who killed me."

"I'd like to ask you some questions, if you don't mind." I stood, pulling Ember to her feet. "But first, I need to tend to my daughter. She's obviously pretty shaken."

"Yeah, yeah. Take all the time you need. I've got eternity," he grumbled.

Roman shot him a dirty look and he ducked away in response.

"Aunt Hattie, I have some of Bev's tea in the cupboard. Can you make Ember a cup of the calming blend?"

I walked Ember out of the kitchen and steered her into the family room.

"I'm sorry," she whispered.

"I know." I reached up and smoothed my hand over the back of her red hair. If I'd learned one thing, it was that sometimes kids deserved a good butt-chewing, and sometimes they learned their lessons the hard way. If the latter was the case, a hug and a little empathy did a lot more good.

I'd just settled her onto the couch and wrapped a blanket around her shoulders, when another interruption came in the form of my sister's voice yelling to me from the front door.

"Shay!" I heard Kiki's heels clicking across the floor as she walked through the living room and into the kitchen. The clicking paused, and I listened to her exchange pleasantries with

Roman, Aunt Hattie and Brock. After a few minutes, she breezed into the family room.

"How did Brock Garrett get here?" she flopped down into the armchair.

"I'll tell you later." I patted Ember's leg. "So, what's up?"

"You'll never guess what amazing news I have!" she squealed.

Brock wandered through the wall behind her and strolled to the other side of the room, taking in the art on the walls and a row of bookshelves.

"Just tell me. I'm too frazzled for games." I said, keeping an eye on Brock.

"Arabel Onassis is putting on a fashion show in Mystic Key!" She clapped her hands together and bounced excitedly.

"Arabel Onassis?" Brock whirled around.

"Yes, do you know her?" Kiki asked.

"No, the name just sounds really familiar. Is she an actress?"

"That's what I thought too." I told him.

"You two are so out of touch." Kiki rolled her eyes and repositioned herself in the chair. "No, she's a designer. And she's phenomenal."

"Where did you hear this?" I asked.

"Oh, I was in Rudolph's shop today and he gave me a personal invitation. Which—let's be honest—as much money as I spend there, he *should* give me a personal invitation." She absentmindedly slid the anchor charm along the silver chain around her neck.

"That's cool, Kiki." I tried, but my voice was completely devoid of enthusiasm.

Aunt Hattie bustled into the room, the smell of chamomile and lavender wafting through the air. After she handed Ember a large mug of steaming hot tea, she took a spot next to Roman on the couch opposite us.

Kiki let her gaze wander, settling on each of us for a moment, before she finally settled on me. "What's been going on around here, anyway?"

"Well, let's see. The cops think Lara Gratz killed Brock even though he had plenty of other enemies. And Ember accidentally summoned him while baking cookies."

She wrinkled her nose. "Wow. that's a lot to happen before lunchtime."

"Tell me about it." I leaned back against the couch and fought the urge to close my eyes.

"They think Lara killed me?" Brock was suddenly interested in the conversation.

I raised my head just enough to see him past the potted cactus next to my spot on the couch. "Yeah. What do you think?"

He worked his jaw, his brow knit together in thought. "She really hated me, I know that much. I suppose it's possible."

"No offense, but a lot of people hated you," I said.

He balked and made a sour face. "That's not true. People liked me. I'm a very charismatic guy."

"You absolutely are not," I scoffed.

He put a hand to his chest and drew back as if he were offended. "How can you say that? I caught the vibes you were laying down the other night. You and your sister both." He motioned to Kiki. "Are you mad I didn't ask for your number or something?"

Kiki and I took one look at each other and burst into laughter.

"What? What's so funny?" He glowered at both of us.

"You're delusional." I wiped at the tears forming in my eyes from the bout of uncontrollable laughter.

"Super delusional." Kiki agreed. "I actually kinda liked that Craig Baldwin guy."

"You did?" I asked.

"He was smart and handsome. He's one of my regulars actually, but we've never had a real conversation before."

"Ah, so that's why he was such a tan vampire. He uses your bronzing service." I recalled that Kiki had told Ember that many of the town's vampires liked to use her spray tanning service. Vampires could go out in the sunlight, they just burned more easily than even the palest of us, so most of them stuck to the shade. Those who were particularly invested in their appearances used Kiki's salon to get that bronzed glow.

"Well, he's a jerk," Brock said. "You think I'm a jerk? He's the jerk."

"It sounded to me like he just didn't appreciate you bullying Ross about trying to buy their new building," I argued.

"Ha!" He rocked back on his heels and shoved his hands in his pockets. "That's not what happened. Not in the slightest. I never bullied Ross. I wouldn't. He's the pack leader, you know. There are lines even I won't cross."

"So why do you think he hates you so much then?" I wasn't necessarily buying Brock's version of events, but I was interested in gathering as much information from him as I could.

"Women. We went after the same ones sometimes." A cheeky grin spread across his face. "And I usually won."

"Probably because you're such a gentleman," Roman's tone oozed sarcasm that went right over Brock's head.

"Yes, I really am." He nodded in agreement.

"Okay, Brock. Tell us what you do remember from that night." I attempted to redirect the conversation.

He scratched at his jawline and looked thoughtful. "I remember chatting with a few people. I remember arguing with Lara. I remember this guy trying to get tough with me." He looked in Roman's direction. "And I remember walking out. But that's it. It's all blank after that."

"Do you remember your conversation with Lara outside the bar? It was on video surveillance."

"No. Did I convince her to come home with me?"

"Maybe," I said under my breath.

His eyes twinkled and he clapped his hands together in delight. "I knew she still had a thing for me. All that passion was just channeled into anger. All she really needed was a good—"

"Shut it, Casanova!" I said loud enough to drown him out. I glanced over at Ember, who was sipping on her tea, her cheeks turning a light shade of pink.

"Who do you think wanted to kill you?" Aunt Hattie asked.

"Truthfully?" He ran his tongue along the inside of jaw. "Probably just some broad that was mad I never called her after a date. But that's broads for ya, right? Women are crazy." He guffawed and I held back the urge to let loose a string of profanities. Aunt Hattie on the other hand, did not.

Once she was done, she was red-faced, and he looked faint.

"I'm not sure we're going to get anywhere until we start talking to people," I said after Aunt Hattie had finally sat back down. "And even then, it might be fruitless. I think we need to call in a big gun."

Roman scrunched up his face. "Who?"

"Lee, of course."

"Who is Lee and why do we need her? Is she cute?" Brock asked.

I groaned and rolled my eyes for added effect. "Lee is a he, for starters. He's also an angel which means he can read people's thoughts. Well, snippets of them."

"Good call." Roman seemed pleased.

"I'm going to see if he's heard any gossip that might help us." I pulled my phone from my back pocket and shot a quick text to Lee. I looked back up to see Brock standing behind Kiki and leering over her in the hope of seeing down her shirt. I threw a blanket at her and narrowed my eyes at Brock. "Watch it," I hissed. He took several steps back and when I was satisfied that he was far enough away from my baby sister, I softened my tone.

"In the meantime, we need you to see if you can remember anything else."

"I've tried. It's just not working."

"I can help." Aunt Hattie said, albeit a bit hesitantly. "I've seen this before. Dozens of times. Sometimes when someone dies tragically, their spirit chooses to forget. It's a self-defense mechanism. But I've pulled memories from ghosts before. I'm sure I can do it again."

"That would be great." A surge of hope washed over me. "Brock, work with Aunt Hattie to try to recover your memories. Roman and I will start working our way down the suspect list."

"And what about me?" Kiki asked.

I opened my mouth to answer when she cut me off. "Oh, wait. I have a date tonight. I can help tomorrow though."

"Who you got a date with?" Brock seemed overly interested.

She beamed and shrugged her shoulders up to her ears. "The bartender from Top Shelf."

I snorted back a laugh. "Kiki, how did you wind up with a date the night Brock was murdered?"

"Well, everyone just took off, and he was stuck there

because he couldn't just leave the bar, you know? So, I kept him company."

"How kind of you," I said in a sarcastic tone.

My phone dinged with a text from Lee. *I've been hearing plenty, but it's all gossip. Want me to narrow my focus to specific folks?*

Yes. I'll call you a little later.

I went to shove my phone back into my pocket when it dinged again. I almost didn't look since I figured it was Lee. He liked to sign off on text conversations with a kissing face emoji. Out of the corner of my eye, I noticed text though and I stopped to read it.

Dad: Hi sweetheart. Just wanted to let you know they brought Brock Garrett's body in today. Funeral is scheduled for Tuesday, so I'll need you in tomorrow. Sorry, I know it's your day off. Love ya.

I guess that meant I'd have to postpone my sleuthing for a day or two. I looked up at Brock, his eyes darting around the room as he took everything in. At least it wouldn't be too difficult to prep him. After all, I'd have a real live—well, not *live,* exactly—model to use.

CHAPTER TEN

*Y*ou know that feeling you get when someone walks into a room, even though you can't see them? That sudden I'm-not-alone feeling? Steve didn't count; his presence was almost an extension of my own. But when I awoke, the sun warming my face from the open window, I felt it before I even opened my eyes.

I lay still, pretending to still be asleep, and praying to every deity I could think of that a masked killer wasn't standing over me.

Good, you're up. I tried to wake you, but it was impossible. That ghost man is here. You might want to cover yourself a bit better, Steve's voice entered my mind.

I opened my eyes and yanked the blanket up to my chin. Brock stood at the foot of my bed, staring down at me with a roguish expression on his face.

"What are you doing in here?" My voice was still hoarse from sleep.

"Nice pajamas," he grinned.

"Ugh. You are disgusting. You *have* to know that." I reached behind my head and grabbed a pillow and chucked it at him. It sailed right through him and out into the hallway. His laughter only angered me more and I sat up, holding the blanket up over my thin nightgown.

"You can't just come in my house and stand at the foot of my bed, creep." I was seething.

Brock simply shrugged and gave me another cheeky smile.

"Fine. You know what?" I used the blanket to cover myself until I reached the chair in my bedroom that held a variety of not-clean-not-dirty clothes and pulled a sweatshirt over my head. A pair of sweatpants fell to the floor and I stuffed my feet into each leg hole and yanked them up in one quick motion. I stomped toward the door, stopping when I reached Brock. "I know a spell to tether you to your body. Is that what you want? Because that's where this is headed." I brushed past him, my shoulder slipping through his, and padded barefoot down the hall. Steve scampered past me and was already waiting on the kitchen counter when I entered.

Instead of following me, Brock appeared in the kitchen, a horrified look on his face. "What do you mean tether?"

"It means she'll tie your spirit to your body. Wherever it goes, you go." Steve yawned and hopped down from the counter once I set his fresh bowl of water and breakfast on the floor.

"No! No, no, no. You can't do that," Brock protested, his hands held up in defeat.

"I can and I will." I slammed the lid to the coffee pot down and jabbed my finger against the power button. The truth was, I knew there was a tethering spell, I just didn't know how to perform it. I was fairly certain that Aunt Hattie did, though, and that was just as good.

"No. Please. I'm sorry." He started to move closer but stopped when he saw the look I was giving him.

"I'll behave. I promise," he whined.

"It's too early for this crap," I muttered, pulling the milk from the refrigerator.

The doorbell rang and I looked at the clock on the microwave.

"And a visitor at seven a.m. It's too early for *that* crap too." I mumbled to myself as I headed for the front door. I used the peephole to see what kind of monster rang people's doorbells at seven in the morning on a Sunday, and was surprised to see my brother standing on the front porch.

I pulled open the door but didn't wait to greet him before I started back to the kitchen. "Coffee?" I asked over my shoulder.

"Sure," he said, following me just until he reached the kitchen table. I busied myself with pouring two cups of coffee and preparing them the way each of us liked. I couldn't help but notice he'd brought his laptop with him. He opened it up and began moving his fingers across the mousepad.

"Shay? You're not going to tether me, right?" Brock asked quietly.

"Who's here?" Matt craned his neck to see into the kitchen.

"Brock Garrett," I answered, carrying two steaming cups of coffee to the table.

Matt raised his eyebrows in surprise, and I planted myself in the chair next to him.

I lifted my coffee mug to my lips. "He doesn't know anything," I added, before taking a sip of the divine liquid.

Brock moved into view and shifted his weight uncomfortably. "Hello, officer."

"Uh … hello." Matt still looked stunned.

"I would've told you he showed up yesterday, but I thought we weren't talking about the case."

He furrowed his brow and I cut him off before he could launch into one of his lectures. "I'm kidding. I didn't call you because, like I said, he doesn't remember anything, and he doesn't seem to think anyone disliked him. He's sort of a useless witness, frankly."

"Hey!" Brock drew his brows down and slammed his fists on his hips in protest.

I ignored him and continued. "Aunt Hattie is working with him to see if he can recover some of his memories."

"Okay … okay, that's good." Matt started to nod as if the reality of what I'd said was finally settling in.

"So, dear brother, why are you here at such an ungodly hour?" I asked, taking a long sip of my coffee.

"I need to ask you some more questions about the night Brock died."

"Ah … so you want my help." I made sure he caught the satisfied smile on my face.

"It's not help, exactly. You're a witness after all." He shifted in his chair and focused on his laptop screen.

"Mmhm. Call it what you want, but we know the truth. Right, Brock?" I said, my eyes still fixed on Matt.

"Yes, ma'am," Brock said a little too quickly.

Matt's gaze slid up from his computer, and a suspicious look clouded his features.

"I threatened to tether him to his body," I said.

"Oh, yeah. She'll do it too," Matt said, a small grin tugging at the corner of his mouth. He turned his laptop screen so I could see it and grabbed the cup of coffee I'd given him.

"Hey Brock, your body is at the funeral home. Why don't you go over and check on yourself?" I encouraged.

"But you guys are talking about who killed me. I want to listen." He looked back and forth between Matt and me expectantly.

"That's fine. I saw Aunt Hattie arriving when I was on my way over. I'm sure she'll take good care of you. She only draws inappropriate pictures on a body's face once in a while."

Sheer horror overtook Brock's features and suddenly, he was gone.

"Why didn't you want him here, anyway?" Matt asked.

"Because he won't be helpful. At least not at this stage. He's a narcissistic pig. He thinks everyone liked him and every woman was in love with him. He'll only lead us in the wrong direction."

Seemingly satisfied with my answer, Matt pulled up a document on his laptop screen. "This is my suspect list. The names in green have been cleared. They were seen in the bar during the window of time that Brock was murdered. The names in yellow—"

"Wait. I know it's early and I haven't had enough coffee yet, but I'm confused. Why are you showing me this? Just yesterday you were adamant that you couldn't talk to me about the case, and now you're going over your suspect list with me."

He let out a deep breath and leaned back in his chair. "Because you're one of three people who were there that night that I trust explicitly. I already talked with Roman, but I know the two of you weren't together all night, which means you spoke with different people and saw different things. Besides that, you're observant. You pick up on things a lot of people don't. So, I need your help, too. As much as it pains me to admit it."

I tried to fight the smile tugging at the corners of my mouth. "What about Kiki?"

"Kiki is ... Kiki. The only people she can vouch for are you, Roman, and some panther shifter whose name she can't remember."

"That sounds about right."

He turned his attention back to his laptop. "As I was saying, the names in green are cleared. The names in yellow are folks that don't check every box, but they check enough that I'm not ready to eliminate them just yet. The names in red are people that are high on my suspect list."

"I see Lara's name is bolded as well." I pointed out.

"Chief Leach, for whatever reason, has his mind made up about her. I'm not ready to cut her from the list, but I'm not as convinced as he is, either."

"Okay, then let's talk about some of these other names." I scanned the list of names highlighted in red.

"Talk to me about Kara Brewer. Did you interact with her at all that night?"

"No, but I did see her keeping a close eye on Brock and she seemed to follow him around a bit. I did see him talking to her though, so he didn't appear to be afraid of her. Not that that means much. Is she a vampire though?"

"No, which is why her name is in yellow and not in red. Same with Morty Mortenson."

"Mr. Mortenson?" I was surprised to hear his name was on Matt's radar.

"Yeah. I guess someone took a bat to Brock's car a couple of weeks ago. Slashed the tires too. He took it into Morty's shop to get it fixed and then he stiffed him. Morty's been trying to get the money he's owed, but Brock kept putting him off, I guess."

"Wow. That's a crappy thing to do."

"Tell me about it," Matt shook his head in disgust.

My front door slammed closed and Matt and I looked at each other.

"Who's here?" he asked.

"No idea. Either someone that doesn't feel the need to knock or someone who's come to kill me. Those are the only types of people who just let themselves in."

I heard the click of heels on the floor and Kiki rounded the corner a few seconds later and came to a halt. "Oh, you're up." She sounded surprised.

"Yeah, but why would you come over and let yourself into my house if you didn't think I was?"

She had a deer caught in the headlights look, her eyes wide and her jaw slack.

"Kiki …" I drew out her name.

She sighed and placed her hands on her hips. "Fine. I wanted to borrow that black A-line dress of yours. The one with the lace sleeves and sweetheart neck."

"For what?" I asked.

"For the fashion show!" She shook her head, exasperated that I didn't remember.

"So why would you sneak in and take it? Why not just ask?" Matt asked what we were both thinking.

"Because I was afraid she might say no." She lowered her voice as if I wouldn't be able to hear her. "She used to get really mad when I'd borrow her stuff. Like, *really* mad."

I rolled my eyes. "Kiki, we aren't teenagers anymore. You can borrow whatever you like."

She bounced up on her toes and clapped excitedly. "Yay! Thanks, Shay!" She spun around and raced for the staircase.

"Don't you dare spill anything on it or I'll use one of my best curses on you!" I called after her.

Matt gave me an amused smile and I shrugged. "Some things never change."

"Don't I know. All right, back to the suspects."

I scanned his list and a name jumped out at me. "Why is Arabel Onassis on there? Was she at the bar that night?"

"I'm not sure. As you know, everyone had to sign in when they arrived. Her name was on the list, but no one recalls talking to her and no one really knows what she looks like, so we don't know for sure if she was there or not."

"It seems a little odd that she would've gone but not spoken to a single person, doesn't it?" I asked.

"Who?" Kiki came back into the room with my dress draped over her shoulder.

"That fashion designer lady. Arabel Onassis," I answered.

Kiki's eyes grew wide and her voice raised an octave. "She was there? At Top Shelf?"

"Maybe," Matt shrugged a single shoulder.

"Do you know what she looks like?" I figured if anyone in the room did, it would've been Kiki.

She nodded emphatically. "There are plenty of pictures of her online from the fashion shows she's attended." She hurried over and shoved herself between Matt and I. Her perfectly manicured nails tapped against the keyboard, and after a few seconds, a handful of images popped onto the screen.

She enlarged one of a catwalk and just behind it were a handful of people staring up at the model from their seats.

"That's her." She pointed to a woman with a short black bob and black sunglasses so large they covered most of her face. She was dressed head to toe in black, and a huge sunhat sat atop her head. She didn't appear to be having a good time, at least not according to the scowl etched on her face.

"You can't really see what she looks like," Matt mused.

"She likes her privacy," Kiki replied. "She always wears those big sunglasses and a floppy hat so no one can ever see what she really looks like."

"Hmm … so, if she was at the bar without them, it would be hard for anyone to recognize her. She could've even given people a false name," Matt surmised.

"What would be the point though? Why would she even be there?" I asked.

"That's the big question," he said, drumming his fingers on the edge of his keyboard.

"What if it was just a prank though?" Kiki tapped her chin with her finger. "What if someone put her name on there as a joke since they knew she was in town?"

"That's a possibility too. I'll take a look at the surveillance tape again and see if anyone with a similar description catches my eye," Matt said.

"You could just go talk to her," I pointed out. "She's staying at Lettuce Inn."

"I know. I've been trying to track her down. I've stopped by twice and I've gone by Rudolph's store hoping to catch her, too. She's a busy woman, it seems. I did leave a voicemail on her cell phone. She returned my call, but I missed it."

Speaking of, Kiki's cell phone rang, and she checked to see who was calling. "Ugh. It's the salon. I swear, they can't manage for a single day without me."

She tapped on the screen and rolled her eyes, offering Matt and I a tiny wave before she strutted out of the kitchen.

Matt and I sat in silence, both studying his long list of suspects.

"Craig Baldwin seemed to have a very low opinion of Brock," I said, noting his name in red.

"Yeah, I interviewed him once already and he made no

effort to hide that fact. Ross Burkman alibied him … sort of. He seemed a little foggy on the time he said he was talking to Craig. But then Matthias Sharpe said he was actually talking to Ross at ten-fifteen, and their conversation was interrupted at exactly ten thirty-five when his wife called and asked him to swing by the store on his way home."

"What are you assuming the time of death was? What's your timeline?"

"We know Brock left the bar at ten and you called me at ten-forty. So, the window of time is incredibly small, which makes me think someone had this planned ahead of time."

"Yeah, and unfortunately the only people that I can safely say I was with during that window were Roman, Morty Mortenson, and I spotted Kiki talking to some guy, but I'm not sure who he was. So, I'm less helpful than you'd hoped I would be."

"Shay … what about Gretchen Gratz?"

I let out a deep sigh. "I know. Her name has crossed my mind too, as much as I hate to admit it."

"I mean, there are only so many vampires in town, and since we know it was a vampire based on the venom we found …"

"And she didn't exactly have a great relationship with Brock," I concluded.

"Exactly. But her motive is still not as solid as Lara's. They both were sick of him pestering them, but Lara had a personal relationship with him and we all know how those can complicate things."

"Did they have an alibi?" I asked, the conversation I'd had with them outside the inn springing to the forefront of my mind.

"Lara said after her confrontation with Brock outside the bar, she went for a walk to cool off. Gretchen says she went with her. However, the security tape shows Lara alone and no sign of Gretchen."

"Maybe she joined up with her after the camera was obstructed?"

"I mean, anything is possible, but it doesn't look good. The evidence is stacking up against Lara, frankly."

"Are you going to arrest her?" I asked.

"Let's just say that if we don't find a more likely suspect soon, there won't be much else I can do for her."

CHAPTER ELEVEN

I ran back into the kitchen to grab the travel mug full of coffee that I'd forgotten and nearly tripped over Steve. He hissed and scrambled out of the way.

"Is everything okay in there?" Ember called out from the family room.

"Your mother's only trying to kill me." Steve scampered out of the kitchen and raced toward Ember's voice.

"So just another Sunday, then?" she quipped just as I passed behind the back of the couch. She was curled up with a cup of hot tea and Tito snoring peacefully in her lap.

"Very funny." I ruffled the top of her head and she ducked away.

"I shouldn't be long. Just a few hours."

"Take your time. I'm just binging Supernatural all day before the new season starts." She pressed a button on the remote and the scene on the TV sprang to life.

I started for the door when she called out, "That ghost … Brock. He's not going to show up while you're gone, is he?"

I stopped and turned back to face her. "No. I'll keep him

occupied at the funeral home today. I'm sure he'll want a say in every minor detail."

She smiled and went back to watching Sam and Dean Winchester banter on TV, and I let out a deep breath, steadying myself for the day ahead.

~

MY DAD HAD ALREADY FINISHED EMBALMING BROCK BY THE time I arrived and was snoring away in the chair behind his desk.

I decided not to wake him and slipped into the preparation room as quietly as possible. Brock's body was laid out on the table, and I was pleased to see my father had already dressed him. His ghost stood in front of my supply station examining tubes of lipstick.

"You're not putting any of this makeup stuff on me, are you?" he asked before I'd even managed to shut the door.

"Some of it." I hung my purse on the wall hook and grabbed a new plastic surgical gown from the closet. I pulled the cap down over my hair next and saved the gloves for last.

"What's all that for?" He eyed me suspiciously.

I picked up my airbrush gun from the supply table and began prepping it.

"It's mostly to protect me." I barely got the words out before he launched into another question.

"What are you doing with that thing?"

I closed my eyes and let out a deep breath through my nose. "Brock, do you want to look good or do you want to ask me a million questions? Because you can't have both."

"Okay, okay. Sorry. I'll shut up."

"Good." I muttered, unbuttoned the top three buttons on the

dress shirt his body was wearing. "And don't make any gross comments," I added, attempting to head off the inevitable.

"You're only undressing me. What comment could I possibly have to make about that?" A smile played at the corners of his mouth and I rolled my eyes, turning my attention back to my work. I stuffed a plastic bib around the collar of his shirt to prevent any staining from the makeup, but when I reached the side of his neck, I gasped in shock.

I felt him come up to stand beside me. "Yeah, pretty nasty bite, isn't it?"

"I don't know what I was expecting it to look like, but that's … not it." I bent at the waist to get a closer look. "It almost looks like it's infected or something." The two puncture wounds in his neck were quite red and given that Brock was dead, I would've expected to see them with a purplish tint indicative of bruising.

I leaned in a little closer and lightly touched one of the marks with my finger to see if it was flush against the rest of his neck. "These are going to be tough to cover, but I think I can do it."

I pulled my finger back, then stood and reached over and grabbed a jar of modeling clay. There was purple goo smeared on the side of the jar, and I stopped to try to deduce where it had come from. I hadn't used glitter glue on a body in weeks, and even then, it had been blue and pink. I searched the counter for the culprit and realized that I'd gotten it on my finger too.

"Gross. What is this stuff?" I griped, picking my way through the jars and tubes scattered there.

"I don't know. But you've gotten it all over my neck too." Brock motioned to his body.

I glanced over to see that he was, in fact, right. "What in shifter's sake …" I muttered, moving closer to the body and leaning down to examine it again. It took a few seconds before I saw the purple goo ooze from his puncture marks.

I shrieked and jumped back, slamming into my supply table and knocking a handful of items to the floor. After I'd recovered, I looked at Brock's body again and, overcome with disgust, I bolted for the door. I came barreling out of the preparation room just as my dad was coming in, and I slammed into him hard enough that it knocked me back onto my butt on the floor.

"What's wrong?" he asked, reaching down to help me up.

"There's purple stuff coming out of his bite marks," I choked out.

My dad's eyes searched mine for a moment as if he were having trouble wrapping his mind around what I was saying. After a full beat, he left me in the hallway to go see for himself.

I stood there in the hall, my stomach doing flips as I waited for my dad to emerge.

"Shay?" he finally called out after what felt like an eternity.

"Yeah?" I called back in a shaky voice.

"Call your brother!"

MATT HAD BEEN AT THE STATION WATCHING THE SURVEILLANCE footage with Chief Leach, and the two had made it to the funeral home in five minutes flat. I stood out front, too creeped out to go back inside just yet.

Aunt Hattie had seen the police car fly up Shadow Lane, and she'd hurried over to make sure everyone was okay. While we waited for my dad, Matt, and Chief Leach to join us outside, I'd told Aunt Hattie what I'd seen. She'd been especially quiet afterward, almost like she was deep in thought.

The door to the funeral home swung open and all three men appeared, matching expressions of worry and confusion masking each of their faces.

"So?" I asked anxiously. "What do you think that stuff is?"

Chief Leach ignored me and addressed my dad instead. "We'll let you know as soon as we get the test results back, but I wouldn't worry. I doubt it's harmful unless it's injected."

"What is it?" I asked again.

"Some kind of venom finding its way out of the body," my dad answered.

"But … vampire venom doesn't do that." I looked from my dad to Matt. "You never tested the venom in the first place, did you?"

Matt cast his gaze downward and shook his head slowly.

"Are you kidding me?" I nearly exploded.

Chief Leach placed his hands on his hips and squared his shoulders. "Why would we? What else around here has venom?"

"What else has venom?" I nearly spat the question.

"Snakes, for one." Aunt Hattie glowered down at him.

"Exactly. You've been looking for a vampire this whole time. What if it's a snake shifter? Or someone that enchanted a snake to do their dirty work?" I shook my head in disgust. "This is unbelievable."

"Pretty shoddy police work." Aunt Hattie agreed.

"You better watch your tone." Chief Leach glared up at Aunt Hattie. "Don't forget who's in charge around here."

"How could I? You're making a real name for yourself proving to everyone that a monkey could do better."

"Aunt Hattie." My dad placed his hand on her shoulder, and I heard him whisper, "Bev is making pot roast tonight and if I have to miss it to come bail you out of jail, I'll never forgive you."

She set her mouth in a hard line and her nostrils flared, but she didn't say anything else.

Matt pulled in a deep breath through his nose and blew it out through his cheeks. "You're correct, Shay, vampire venom doesn't do that. The body just absorbs it. So, we're probably dealing with something else."

"Does that mean you're going to leave Lara alone now?" I narrowed my eyes at Chief Leach.

"I'm not ready to remove anyone from my suspect list. In fact, this only adds to it," he said, his expression smug.

"We're going to test the venom—" Matt started.

"Which you should've done in the first place," I cut in.

He continued despite my outburst. "And once we know exactly what kind of poison it is, we'll have a better idea of how to narrow our search."

"Except literally, anyone could use a snake," I pointed out. "It doesn't have to be a snake shifter."

"While that's true, enchanting a snake isn't something just anyone could do. That would be reserved for those of us with certain types of magic."

"Witches, for one." Chief Leach looked up at me with his scrunched-up beady eyes.

"What about gorgons?" Brock was suddenly standing between Chief Leach and I, though Leach couldn't see him.

"Oh, yes! Gorgons. I hadn't thought of them!" I said a little too excitedly.

Matt rubbed his chin. "That's actually a good angle to look at. We don't have many around here though. Brock, did you have any run-ins with a gorgon recently?"

A lopsided grin formed on his face. "I've never called it a run-in before, but I suppose that phrase works."

Matt looked at me, confused.

"I'm assuming he's making some inappropriate joke." I rolled my eyes.

"There's a … lady of the night," Brock started, "that I see every once in a while. Her name's Darla."

"Darla what?" I asked.

"Look, honey, I don't usually get the last names of the … ladies of the night that I spend time with."

"Stop saying lady of the night," Aunt Hattie grumbled. "We all know what you mean."

"Do you know how we can find her?" Matt asked.

Brock furrowed his brow and after a beat he said, "I usually see her down at the old bar by the dock."

"Yikes. That place is a real dive," I said.

He shrugged. "Sometimes I get tired of the kind of women in regular places. The Freaky Tiki has the kind of girls you definitely don't take home to mom."

"Thanks." Matt was scribbling in his notebook. "Any others?"

"Not that I recall. I'm not really into gorgons. Darla's just special." He winked as if there was some joke that Matt was supposed to get.

Matt nodded and stuffed his notepad back in his pocket at the exact moment his cell phone rang. He whipped it from his duty belt and answered.

"This is Graves."

"The venom was purple," I said. "What kind of snake has purple venom, anyway?"

"Got it. I'm with the Chief. We're on our way." Matt shoved his phone back on his belt.

"We've got another one." he said, already turning to head to his car.

"Another body?" I asked.

"Another victim. This one's still alive, but he's in a coma. Same marks, though."

Chief Leach waddled after Matt, trying to keep up.

"Who is it?" I asked. The sudden realization that I hadn't spoken to Roman yet that day sent an unexpected wave of panic over me.

"Craig Baldwin!" Matt called out just before jumping inside the driver's seat of his car and slamming the door closed.

CHAPTER TWELVE

$\mathcal{I}$ stood there dumbfounded while I watched my brother and Chief Leach speed down Shadow Lane and out of sight.

Once they were gone, I realized Brock was chuckling to himself.

"Why are you laughing?"

"Serves him right, is all."

"Brock, no one deserves what happened to you or to Craig. Don't be a jerk." I scolded him with the best mom tone I could muster. It must've worked, because he shrank back and mumbled an apology.

"It does change things, though," I said.

My dad glanced over at me as we walked back up the sidewalk. "What do you mean?"

"Well, Craig and Brock were enemies, and frankly, Craig was high on my personal list of suspects. But now that they've both been attacked, it stands to reason that they share a common enemy as well. It might be easier to find out who did this now because we can narrow the suspect list even further."

"Who hated you both?" Aunt Hattie asked.

"I'm telling ya, it's probably some crazy broad that doesn't like rejection. Craig and I are both ladies' men."

"Do you know if he ever had … what do you call them? Dates? With Darla?"

"I couldn't say. I didn't ask her about her clients, and I doubt she would've told me anyway. She's very professional and good at keeping client confidentiality."

"Well, I'm going to pay her a visit," I said, pulling the door open so I could go back inside and grab my things.

"Be careful, Shay. She's a gorgon, after all," Aunt Hattie warned.

"I know. I'm not going alone."

"You're taking that big druid with you, aren't you?" Brock asked. "Why don't you two just go out and get it over with."

"What are you talking about?" Heat rushed to my cheeks.

"It's plain as day to anyone with two eyeballs." Brock smirked and looked at Hattie to back him up. "You two have the hots for each other."

"I don't have time for this." I spun around and headed back inside, the warmth in my cheeks intensifying. Once I made it to my belongings, which someone had placed in the office, I pulled out my cell and saw that I'd missed a call from Roman.

I hit the button to call him back and he answered almost immediately.

"Hey," he said, relief tinging his voice. "It's about time you called me back. I've been staring at my phone like a girl without a prom date."

"Yeah, things have been crazy around here." I went over the events of the morning for him while I gathered my things.

"This is a huge development." He huffed out a deep breath. "It makes the reason I called seem kind of dumb."

"I'm sure that's not true," I argued.

"Well, I was just thinking ... remember Brock's neighbor? That cranky old lady? She kept yammering on about how she was being stalked, but what if she wasn't the one being stalked, but Brock was? What if she had it right, but it just wasn't about her?"

"Wow. That's actually a serious possibility. Maybe we should go talk to her."

"That's what I was thinking. And now that we know Craig Baldwin is the second victim, maybe we should chat with his neighbors, too, and see if they saw anything strange."

"That's a great plan. And after that, we can swing by Freaky Tiki and chat with Darla."

He sucked in a deep breath.

"Don't be scared," I said, trying to reassure him. "Gorgons are nice. Most of them, anyway. You only need to worry if you cross them. You haven't crossed any gorgons, have you?"

"No, ma'am," he said. "Not that I know of, anyway."

"All right then. It's a date." I breezed through the main hallway toward the front door and winced at my own word choice.

"I'm going to put in a call with my buddy at the medical examiner's office. I want to know when they get the test results back on the venom. Then I'll swing by and pick you up," he said.

"See you soon." I hung up the phone and quickened my pace, mumbling to myself. "So much for taking a few days off from sleuthing."

MOIRA MEEKS WAS STANDING IN HER FRONT YARD WITH A

watering can in one hand and a shovel in the other when we pulled up outside of her house. She squinted, trying to see into the car. Once Roman and I emerged, she dropped both items and scowled.

"What do you two want?" she called out before we'd even managed to make it through the front gate.

"We wanted to talk to you about your stalker," Roman answered, holding the wrought-iron gate open for me to pass through.

"At least someone does," she muttered, yanking her gardening gloves off and tossing them down.

"Can you tell us exactly what you told the police?" I asked.

She crossed her arms over her chest and scrunched up her nose, and I got the distinct impression that it might hurry this whole thing along if I let Roman do the talking.

She let out a deep sigh. "About a week or so ago, I see movement outside. In the bushes right over there." She pointed behind us to the row of hedges that separated her property from Brock's. "I went out to investigate thinking it might be an animal. They like to get into my garden. Anyway, I must've scared them off that first night because I didn't find anyone. The next night, I saw a figure dressed in all black skulking around. They were crouched low to the ground, but I saw 'em. I called the cops right away, but by the time they got here, whoever it was, was long gone. The night after, I see the bushes moving again so I go out with a flashlight this time and I swear to you, I saw eyes."

She paused to take a breath and pointed to the row of hedges again. "Right there. Smack dab in the middle, I saw eyes staring back at me. Then the hedges rustled again, and they were gone. That's when I called the cops for the second time. Every night, they came out and looked around my yard, but they told me they didn't find any evidence that someone had been out here."

"No footprints?" Roman walked along the row of hedges that lined the property and studied the ground.

"Nah. That's what was confusing. It's all dirt right there."

"Did you see the figure in your yard or Brock's?" I asked.

She looked a bit taken aback by my question. "Well, Brock's, but they were after me." She jabbed her thumb toward her chest. "They were looking at my house when I caught them."

"Probably because they saw your flashlight bouncing around outside." I considered this new information. "Roman, are there footprints on the other side of the hedge?"

He hurried down the edge of Moira's yard and around the other side, ducking under the crime scene tape. I watched him, holding my breath as he slowly walked along the hedges examining the dirt. When he reached the spot that Moira had pointed to earlier, he stopped suddenly.

"Well, sweet sorcery," I heard him mutter. His head snapped up and I saw the disbelief play in his eyes. "There are a handful of footprints over here."

"I knew it!" I couldn't contain my excitement.

"Yeah, because they were hiding in his yard to spy on me." Moira was still determined to convince us that she was the one with the nightly visitor.

"They're … small." Roman sounded surprised.

"What do you mean?" I tried to bounce up on my tiptoes to see over the hedge, but I was still too short.

"Come around to this side and you'll see what I mean." He advised.

I could feel Moira hot on my heels as I rushed to meet Roman.

He had knelt down next to the dirt, and I saw right away what he meant. "Those don't look like they belong to a man," I said. "Or at least not an average-sized one."

"No, they don't. They're far too small."

"Well, it wasn't a kid. I saw the figure. It was an adult." Moira adjusted her glasses.

"An elf, maybe?"

Roman looked up at me. "It's possible. Or maybe a petite woman."

"Or just someone with tiny feet. You two are reading too much into this." Moira suddenly turned and headed back toward her house. "And by the way, you tell that brother of yours what you found. If two knuckleheads like you can find evidence that the police can't, then I'm afraid for the safety of this town."

"I'll call Matt from the car." Roman stood and fished his cell phone out of his pocket. He snapped a few pictures of the footprints first. "Craig Baldwin's place is close."

"And then we'll hit up Freaky Tiki?"

"It's like you're just dying to go there," he teased. "It's all you can talk about."

"Stop." I gave his arm a playful slap and cringed at how Kiki-like that was.

"You okay?"

"Yeah, let's hurry though." I turned and started toward the car. "We've got a killer to catch."

CHAPTER THIRTEEN

*C*raig Baldwin was one of those vampires that had old money. He'd been around long enough that he'd acquired enough wealth to live comfortably well past my lifespan and probably my great-grandchildren's too.

His house sat at the end of a winding road, flanked on either side by the most magnificent palm trees I'd ever seen.

"It's weird. You don't see palm trees up here much. They're mostly down by the resort," I said to Roman.

"Most of us like to keep the town separate from the vacation vibe down near the resorts. That way, we don't get sick of either, but I have a feeling Craig Baldwin is really into the island thing. I mean, you saw his tan."

I snickered at the memory.

"No one that wants a natural tan goes that overboard. The man looked like an Oompa Loompa."

We pulled up in front of the first mansion on the hill, and I spotted a Jaguar in the driveway.

"Does he live alone?" I asked.

"He does, but he has a married couple living here that handles all the upkeep."

Before we'd even had a chance to knock on the front door, it swung open and a cheerful older woman in a turquoise bikini greeted us. Her gray hair was pulled up on top of her head and the strings around her neck were digging into her skin in a gallant attempt at keeping her large bosom covered.

"Can I help you?" She smiled brightly and I noticed a man passing by the foyer with what appeared to be little more than a piece of cloth covering him.

Roman and I both looked at each other, slightly confused by the way we were being greeted at the house of the man who was nearly dead in the hospital.

"Uh, we were hoping to ask you some questions," Roman stumbled over the words. "About Craig Baldwin."

The woman's face fell, and she shook her head, "Such a terrible shame. I'm the one who found him, you know."

"What's going on? Who's here, Betty?" The older gentleman joined the woman without making any effort to throw a towel or something around himself first.

"Nice Speedo," I said.

He looked down at his tiny suit, an ocean blue with little red crabs all over it and back up at me. "Thanks. Betty here got it for me. She said it makes me look sexy."

"I'm sure she did." I cast a sidelong glance at Roman, who wore a lopsided grin.

"These folks were just asking about Mr. Baldwin," Betty told the man.

"Oh, yes. Terrible, terrible thing to happen to such a nice fella."

"You mentioned you found him?" I prodded.

"Oh, yes. Well, see Mr. Baldwin is always sitting at the table with a newspaper drinking his first glass of juice at exactly six a.m. every single morning for the past thirty years that we've been with him."

"Wait. I don't mean to interrupt, but you said juice."

"Oh, that's just what we call it around here. I don't like saying blood if I don't have to," Betty explained. "Anyway, so he never came down this morning. Around ten or so, I went up to check on him and that's when I found him. He was up against the wall over his bed." She shuddered and the man put his arm around her shoulders.

"You know, vampire blood is fatal to other vampires," the man said. "Might be a dead vampire somewhere that no one has found yet."

"You mean because he was bitten? You think they took his blood?" Betty looked horrified at the idea.

The man only shrugged. "It's possible."

"It is. I hadn't considered that theory." I looked up at Roman who nodded in agreement. I decided it was best not to let them know that it was possible the attacks weren't done by a vampire. I was certain that information hadn't been made public, and I was trying to help, not hinder, the case.

"One last question. Have either of you seen anything strange around here the last few days? Maybe someone on the property or a visitor Mr. Baldwin might've had?"

Betty and the man both looked thoughtful for a few moments.

"Even if it doesn't seem important, it might be," I urged, hoping they'd at least give us something.

"He did have a … lady friend over last night." Betty's cheeks grew pink.

"Well, that's big. Did you see what she looked like?" I asked.

"No, but she was gone around midnight. I heard her leave, and Mr. Baldwin came downstairs afterward to get a glass of juice."

"And I locked up around two," the man added.

"Mr. Baldwin has a lot of … friends." Betty was trying to be diplomatic. "So, it wasn't out of the ordinary at all."

A figurative light bulb must've gone on over the man's head, because he held up his finger, "He did have an argument with Ross a few days ago."

"Do you know what they argued about?" Roman asked.

"Brock Garrett, I think. Mr. Baldwin didn't care for him much, and Mr. Burkman wasn't getting any sympathy from him about the death of one of his pack members. Then they argued about some business stuff, I think. I'm not sure, as Mr. Baldwin shut his office door."

"Does anyone besides the three of you have a key to the house?" Roman asked.

"No, sir. Just Mr. Baldwin, Betty, and myself. Mr. Baldwin doesn't like giving out keys because he doesn't want to ever have to deal with changing the locks."

"That's helpful. Thank you," I said.

Roman and I headed back to the car and my mind raced with new possibilities.

He started the car and turned to look at me, a smile spreading across his face.

"I know. He had crabs on his banana hammock," I burst into laughter.

After our fits of laughter died down, Roman pulled out of the driveway. "So, the tiki bar?"

"Yes, but it's still early. I'm not sure the place will be that busy just yet. We probably have a better chance of running into Darla if we wait a bit. Coffee first?"

"Coffee it is."

"Good. I'd like to see if Ross Burkman is around Brews Brothers today. I have some questions for him."

As expected, Brews Brothers was busy with both the after-church crowd and those lucky people who got to sleep in late on a Sunday. The barista had asked us to wait at a table while she let Ross know we were there. I sipped on my latte and bounced my leg, staring at the door that led to the back office. After less than five minutes, Ross Burkman emerged looking like he hadn't slept in days. He trudged over to our table, and I was surprised by the dark circles under his eyes and the new, unkempt gray beard that he was sporting.

He pulled an empty chair over to our table and lowered himself slowly. "I'm the owner."

"Uh, yeah, we know. We met you the other night at the Business Leaders of Mystic Key event. I'm Shay Graves and this is Roman Daniels." I looked at Roman, who had his brow knit together as he studied Ross.

"Oh, of course." Ross smacked his forehead with his palm. "Forgive me. It's been … it's been a very long week. I do remember you both though. Your family owns the funeral home and you own the Mystic Key Tribune." He pointed at each of us, respectively.

"I'm sorry about your friends," I offered.

His face fell and he chewed on the inside of his cheek for a moment before he spoke. "You heard about Craig Baldwin then? Guess I shouldn't be surprised. News travels fast around here."

"Well, to be honest, I was with my brother when he got the call. He's the deputy."

"Oh, sure. I've spoken with him a few times now," Ross said.

I figured beating around the bush wouldn't do any of us any favors, so I got straight to it. "Ross, I don't want to upset you, but we spoke with Craig's employees just a little while ago and they mentioned you and he had an argument the other day."

Ross's expression hardened and he stood abruptly. "Are you really here, in my establishment, accusing me of something?" He was wild-eyed now, and he bent at the waist to look me in the eye. "One of my friends is dead and the other is close." He spat the words out at me, and I was starting to regret cutting the chase.

Roman jumped up from his seat so fast that it fell over, clattering against the floor. The coffee shop grew silent as everyone turned to see where the noise had come from. Roman placed a hand against Ross's chest, and I watched as Ross relaxed and the hard look faded from his face. His posture changed, and he slumped his shoulders forward and lowered himself back into his chair. "I'm sorry. It's been a very stressful week and I shouldn't have taken it out on you."

I felt a wave of guilt wash over me. "No, I understand. I'm sorry my question was so abrupt. It's just that we want to find out what's happened to your friends before it happens to someone else."

Ross widened his eyes, "I hadn't even considered that possibility."

Roman leaned forward and propped his forearms on the table. "I think you should. Especially since you have them both in common."

"You think *I'm* a target?" His mouth fell open in shock.

"I just think you need to be extra careful is all."

Ross nodded and let out a deep breath. "To answer your question, Craig and I, we argue all the time. We're like brothers. I know that might sound a little funny—a wolf shifter and a vampire being best friends—but we've known each other a long time. We argue, but we get over it after about five minutes. We don't see eye to eye on a lot of things, but there's never been any bad blood between us."

"And Brock? How was your relationship with him?"

Ross looked a little taken aback by the question, but he recovered quickly. "Brock is—was—a member of my pack. He drove me batty sometimes and I had to clean up a lot of his messes, but that's one of the hazards of being in charge, I'm afraid. And since Brock was in my pack, that made us family. You don't always like your family, but you love them."

"I can't argue with that," I said.

"Thanks for talking with us," Roman added.

Ross bobbed his head and rose from his chair. "I better get back to work. It's the only thing keeping me sane right now." He turned and we watched him meander toward his office door.

"I feel bad for him. He looks rough," I said.

"Well, well, well. Look who it is. Thanks for ghosting me," Lee Tucker sauntered over and plopped down in the empty chair.

"Oh, shoot! Lee, I am so sorry!" I had completely forgotten to call him the night before.

"Some wife you are." He tugged at the front of his corduroy suit jacket.

Lee had been my very best friend when I was a kid, and we'd had a pretend wedding in the graveyard once. He liked to use that fact to tease me every chance he got. He was also an angel who had been fired from his job as an Afterlife Chaperone. It was a sore subject due to the fact that he was too passive when it came to convincing human souls to crossover. That's the story anyway. If you ask me, I think it's more likely that he was too snarky and impatient, and they refused to go with him out of sheer protest.

"By the way, what's ghosted mean?" I asked.

"Oh, Shay. Try to keep up with the times, would you? No wonder Ember doesn't think you're cool." He gave my hand a sympathetic pat. "It means you disappeared on me."

"I know. I'm sorry," I apologized again.

"Well, I'll forgive you under one condition." The twinkle in his eye meant he was about to make me agree to something that I did not want to agree to.

"Okay. What is it?"

"I just so happened to score an invitation to the LeBeau Onassis fashion show. Me!" He squealed with delight. "In fact, I'm on my way now, but I had to stop in for a coffee because the drive down to the resort where they're hosting it is one of those where it's so peaceful and beautiful that it just makes you sleepy. And, oh honey, I can't tell you how many times I went to collect a poor soul that had fallen asleep while driving—"

"Lee." I raised my voice just enough that he could hear me over his own. "Focus."

"Right. Sorry. Anyway, I can't get you into the show, but I do have an invite to the after party tonight. And I was told I could bring a plus one. Since there's no Mister Tucker and no *potential* Mister Tucker, I suppose my wife will do." A huge grin spread across his face. "So, will you be my date? It starts at seven."

"You want me to go with you to a party with a bunch of snobby fashion people?"

"Yes!" He bounced excitedly in his chair. "Oh, Roman, I'm

so sorry. Will you be sad if you don't get to come? I might be able to sneak you in."

An amused look played across Roman's features. "No, Lee, I think I'll be all right. Thank you for thinking of me, though."

"Of course. Any friend of Shay's is a friend of mine."

"So, Shay? Will you be my date?"

I groaned and threw my head back for added effect. "Fine. But you have to promise that if there are people there I need you to read, you'll do it."

"Deal." He reached out and shook my hand.

"Alright fine. Then yes, I'd love to be your date. I'll meet you there at seven." My stomach dropped as I realized that I'd just lived out Paige's vision.

"What's wrong? You look pale," Lee held his hand to my forehead.

"I'm fine. I just need some water."

"I'll get it." Roman sprung to his feet and headed toward the counter.

Disappointment sat like a rock in the pit of my stomach, and I silently cursed at myself for thinking Roman might actually ask me out on a date.

"Oh, baby," Lee said in his Southern drawl, his eyes searching mine with sympathy.

"Don't read my thoughts," I said, but without any fight in me to give those words the stern tone they needed.

Lee scooted his chair closer and leaned his head against mine.

"Here you go." Roman placed a bottle of water on the table in front of me. "Are you sure you're okay?"

"I'm fine. We should probably get going down to Freaky Tiki soon though."

"Ew." Lee pulled away from me and scrunched up his face. "Why in the world do y'all want to go down to that pit?"

"There's a gorgon we need to see," I told him, unscrewing the cap on the water bottle.

Lee shivered and made another disgusted face. "You better be careful. Gorgons don't get along with other women too well. You don't want her to whip off her headdress and turn you into stone. Though, you would make a cute statue."

I raised a brow. "I'll let Roman do most of the talking."

"Probably best. You have a habit of saying the wrong thing at the wrong time." Lee winked to let me know he was teasing.

I pretended to lock my mouth and toss the key away.

"You're welcome to join us, Lee," Roman offered.

"Oh, absolutely not. I wouldn't be caught dead going in that place. The riff raff there doesn't take kindly to my type," He scoffed.

"What type? Gay?" I balked, offended on Lee's behalf.

"No, no, no." Lee reached out and squeezed my hand affectionately. "Angel."

"Ohhh," I nodded in understanding.

"What's wrong with angels?" Roman looked back and forth between the two of us.

"We have a reputation for being…"

"Pious. And arrogant," I interjected.

Lee lifted his chin slightly and looked down at the table. "It's an unfair stereotype, but I've had to live with it all my life."

"Oh, you poor thing," I said in a mocking tone and he shot me a playful glare.

"I'd think you might have a little street cred since you're no longer serving as an Afterlife Chaperone," Roman said.

"You would think," Lee sniffed.

"Well, I wish you were coming in case Darla was open enough that you could read her thoughts, but we'll see if we can get anything out of her the old-fashioned way.

Lee stood and bent down to give me a quick peck on the top of my head. "I've got to get to the fashion show, but I'll see you tonight. I'll text you the address. And don't you dare ghost me again, Shay Graves." He wagged his finger at me.

I grinned and held up my right hand. "I wouldn't dream of it."

CHAPTER FOURTEEN

There was nothing tiki-esque about Freaky Tiki aside from the thatched roof that had so many holes in it that it looked like it had been dive-bombed.

"Are you sure you're okay?" Roman asked as we walked down the dock toward the entrance. "You were really quiet in the car."

"Of course. I just have a lot on my mind is all." Like how I was disappointed that Paige's vision wasn't about you and *why* I was disappointed in the first place.

"Okay. Just making sure." He looked at me and smiled but I could see the question in his eyes.

The front of the bar facing the dock was open and even though a soft breeze of fresh air washed over it, the smell of alcohol and stale cigarettes still hit me the second we stepped over the threshold.

A man in his fifties stood behind the bar, cleaning a glass with a rag. He was sans shirt and his hairy chest and beer gut jutted out from the too small leather vest he wore. He was bald, but he made up for it with a long gray beard. He narrowed his eyes at us as we approached the bar.

I placed my hand down on the sticky old wooden bar and pulled it back instantly. The man grunted and stepped back to place the glass on the shelf behind him. That was when I noticed he was a centaur.

"Oh, do you know Troy over at Bar Humbug?" I asked.

He frowned.

"He's a centaur too," I explained.

"Not all centaurs know each other, lady." He shook his head and turned his back to us, busying himself with organizing receipts.

"No, of course. I know that." I felt my cheeks flush. "I just thought it was a funny coincidence that you're both centaurs that bar tend. That's all."

He grunted again but kept working on his receipt organization.

"I'm sorry. I didn't mean to offend you." I was obviously off to a rough start.

He turned back around and rested his hands on the bar, "You think that was offensive? You should spend some time in this hell hole, lady."

He must've read something in my eyes because he burst into a fit of raucous laughter. Once he was done, he shook his head and chuckled a few more times, his belly jiggling in perfect unison with each chortle, "So, what brings two folks like you into a place like this?"

"We're looking for someone, actually," Roman said.

"I'm not sure you'll find 'em. This is the place people come when they don't want to be found." He waggled his eyebrows.

"We aren't police," I said hurriedly.

A wide smile spread across his face and he barked out a

short laugh, "No kiddin', lady. Trust me, I wasn't thinking you were."

"Let's try this another way." I saw the muscle in Roman's jaw twitch. "What would a man do if he were looking for a nice lady to spend the evening with?"

The man furrowed his brow and his eyes darted back and forth between the two of us. I assumed he was trying to work out whether we were an item. He finally said, "Well, if a fella were looking for a nice lady to spend the evening with, I'd say he found her." He nodded his head in my direction. "But if he were looking for uh... something else, he'd go sit down at the end of the bar." His head tilted to the left, but he kept his eyes on us. "He'd also be sure to proceed with caution."

"Thanks," Roman said and we both turned to walk to the darkest corner of the bar.

"Miss," the man called out a bit urgently. "It might be best if you stayed here."

I was slightly stunned by the warning, but Roman gave me an encouraging nod. "I'll keep an eye on you the whole time." He walked away, leaving me standing there with the burly bartender.

I climbed up onto a barstool and dropped my purse down into my lap. "Well, I might as well have a drink then. What do you recommend?"

He gave me a lopsided smile. "I make a pretty good Tidal Wave."

"Okay, I'll try one of those." I watched him blend and pour and when he was done, he placed a drink in front of me that resembled the one Kiki had ordered for me at Top Shelf.

"It usually comes with cherries, but I don't keep fruit out here if I can help it. The heat makes the whole place smell like garbage."

"As opposed to a sweat, booze, and the bottom of an ashtray?"

He let out a deep belly laugh and wagged his finger at me, "You're funny. Mouthy, but funny." He leaned in until his belly rested on the bar and lowered his voice, "Which is exactly why I didn't want you to go down there."

My eyes slid in the direction of the bar where Roman had disappeared to. He'd chosen a seat directly under one of the holes in the roof and the sun cast the perfect light over him. He had his arms crossed over his chest, and he leaned back so far in his chair that I thought it might topple over. I saw a woman's hand resting on the table, but I couldn't make out much else.

I forced myself to stop gawking and turned my attention back to the bartender, "See, I always thought gorgons were supposed to be nice. I had a kindergarten teacher who was a gorgon and she was one of the sweetest ladies."

His mouth curved into a smile, "Yeah, Mrs. Tingle, right? I had her too. Man, she was a sweet lady. But you can't use her as a realistic point of reference. Most gorgons are *not* like Mrs. Tingle."

I took a few sips of my drink and watched him wipe down a few more glasses. "So, how come you didn't ask why we were looking for her?"

"I already know. Brock Garrett, right?" He placed one of the glasses on the shelf behind him and began wiping another. "I thought the cops would come by, but they never did. So, what's your angle? Why are you two here?"

"The police think my friend is guilty and I want to help find the real killer."

"You must be an awfully good friend. I got arrested during a motorcycle trip through Missouri once. My friends were gone by the time I was released the next morning."

"You need better friends."

"I got 'em now," He grinned and took my empty glass. "Mystic Key is a much better place for a guy like me."

"What's your name, anyway?" I asked.

"Chuck."

"So, Chuck, you got any information you think might help me out?"

He tilted his head and studied me for a full minute, "What kind of information are you looking for exactly?"

I leaned forward to rest my chin in my hands and let out a deep sigh. "I'm not sure I even know anymore. See, I thought I knew what I was supposed to be looking for, but now I'm not sure anymore. And that's not *my* fault, by the way. I didn't have all the information. Or, more accurately, I didn't have the *right* information."

"And now you do?"

I snickered and shrugged my shoulders up to my ears. "I think I do, but who knows?"

"I heard it was some kind of vampire-on-vampire crime," Chuck said.

"That's because the police never tested the venom," I blurted out. I clapped my hands over my mouth, but it was too late.

He lifted an eyebrow and let out an exasperated grunt, "I wish I could say that surprised me." He places a second drink in front of me. "Since you're here to see the lady with the snakes on her head, I'm going out on a limb and guessing it wasn't a vampire after all?"

"We don't know for sure yet, but it's a good possibility."

I knew I really shouldn't indulge in a second alcoholic beverage. I needed to keep a clear head, but I didn't want to be rude either. I took a small sip of the fruity drink in front of me, "Do you know any snake shifters on the island?"

"I know a few, but I can't say any of them would have cared enough about a guy like Brock to kill him. Beat him up in the bar? Yeah. But that's about it."

"What about Craig Baldwin? Do you know him?"

"Can't say I do. I've heard Brock whining about him a time or two, but I've never met him myself."

"He was attacked sometime late last night but he survived."

"Well, what's he got to say then?"

"He's in a coma."

"That's too bad. Hope he pulls through."

I nodded and swirled my straw around, mixing the red and yellow liquids together. "One thing I can't quite figure out, though, is how a shifter would've been able to use an enchantment. Brock was stuck to the ceiling and Craig was on the wall above his bed. Shifters usually don't dabble in that kind of magic."

Chuck shrugged, "What if it wasn't just one person?"

"I hadn't considered that possibility. I *had* considered it could be someone with the ability to enchant a snake to do their dirty work though. Know any snake whisperers?"

"Nah, but Matthias Sharpe might. He's really into snakes. He's got a whole house full of 'em."

I perked up at the revelation, "He does?"

"Yeah, I'd ask him if I were you. He might give you some leads."

"And where might I find him?"

"He owns the nursery."

"Oh, well no wonder I've never met him. I'm no good at keeping things alive that don't verbally demand it." I stared down in my drink, trying to remember where I'd heard his name before. "Oh! He was at Top Shelf the night Brock was murdered. I didn't meet him, but Ross Burkman mentioned he had business to discuss with him."

Chuck opened his mouth to say something, but he snapped it shut and pretended to busy himself with wiping down the bar.

I heard the unmistakable clicking of high heels drawing closer and I turned just in time to see a woman sashaying in my direction. A silk wrap in a bright aquamarine color sat on top of her head and I could see the snakes slither against the fabric. Her eyes were an icy gray color and they bore into me with an intensity that was nothing short of frightening. I was afraid to keep staring, but I was more afraid to look away. She breezed past me but stopped just behind my barstool. I felt her lean in, the smell of cheap perfume tickling my nose and the hot air from her breath on the back of my neck.

"You've got a good one there," she said in a raspy voice.

"Sorry?" My mouth suddenly felt dry.

"That man you came in here with. He's a good catch. I'd hang onto him if I were you."

A soft cool breeze caressed my back in the place she'd just been, and I saw her continuing past the bar toward a troll sitting by himself. He looked pleased to see her and she wrapped an arm around his shoulders and whispered something in his ear. I looked back at Chuck who seemed relieved.

"Were you afraid for me?" I asked.

"Maybe a little." He winked and gave me a lopsided grin.

"Well, she was helpful, but she didn't know much more than we do," Roman leaned his hip against the bar and crossed his arms over his chest. He looked down and spotted the drink in front of me. "So, you're just going to sit back and have a few cocktails while I do all the dirty work, huh?"

"I only had one." I straightened my back and looked him

square in the eye to prove I was still completely sober. "Okay, maybe one and a half."

He grinned and pulled his wallet from his back pocket, "What do I owe you, sir?"

Chuck waved him off and scrunched up his face. "Nah. It's on the house."

"Are you sure?" I asked.

"Yeah. That was the first decent conversation I've had around here in a long time."

"Thanks, Chuck. And thanks for the information about Matthias Sharpe. I really appreciate it."

He nodded at both of us, "Good luck."

I hopped down from the barstool and followed Roman back out to the dock. Once we'd almost reached his car, he asked about Matthias.

"Apparently he owns a bunch of snakes. Chuck said he might know someone around town who has the ability to enchant snakes."

"I mean, are we sure Matthias doesn't?" Roman asked.

"No, we aren't. But we're going to find out."

He held the passenger side door open for me and I climbed inside just as he got a call on his cell phone. I watched him walk around the front of the car and once he'd closed his door, he said, "Okay, George, go ahead." He lowered the phone and tapped the screen and a man's voice came through the speaker phone.

"So, we just finished testing the venom and I can guarantee you with one hundred percent certainty that it is *not* from a vampire."

Roman sucked in a breath through his teeth, "Do you know what it is from then?"

"Not yet. I have a snake shifter buddy that I was just talking with and he said he's never seen purple venom before. Then again, it could be from a rare breed of snake."

"All right. Thanks, George."

"Oh, and by the way, you know that sticky stuff that we found on the ceiling and Brock's body?"

Roman and I looked at each other and both shook our heads.

"No, I didn't hear about any sticky stuff."

"Oh, well, we found this weird substance at both the Garrett and Baldwin crime scenes, which means it wasn't likely an enchantment like we first thought."

"So, wait, someone what? Glued them up to the ceiling and wall?"

"Sort of."

"What kind of creature could do that?" I whispered to Roman.

He shook his head, the muscles twitching in his jaw. "Could a snake do that?"

"If it were well evolved enough then, yes, according to my shifter friend. Or a hybrid of some sort."

"Okay. Thanks again. Let me know if you find anything else."

"Will do." George said before the phone beeped to indicate he'd hung up.

"I feel like we're back at square one," I said.

"I know it feels like that. But we aren't. At least we know we can eliminate the vampires. And, if you think about it, we've actually narrowed our suspect pool substantially."

I smiled up at him. "You're always looking at the upside, aren't you?"

"I try." He shrugged and leaned forward to start the car. "So, where to next?"

I checked the time on the dashboard. "I'd really like to

swing by the nursery and talk with Matthias Sharpe, but I need to get home and get ready for that stupid party I promised Lee I'd go to."

"I can go see him alone, if you want. And then we can reconnect later and go over everything. Hopefully you'll learn something at this party. I'd take even the weakest lead at this point."

"Yeah, me too. Okay," I agreed. I didn't like being left out of Roman's visit to see Matthias, but I knew it made more sense for us to split up. "Sounds like a plan."

CHAPTER FIFTEEN

"I swear this dress fit a few months ago." I struggled to pull the black satin dress down over my backside.

"Well, you've gone through a divorce since then." Steve was stretched out on my bed, watching a baking show on TV.

"So?" I grunted, finally getting the dress down over my butt and hips.

"So, you stress eat."

"Gee. Thanks for pointing that out," I said in a sarcastic tone.

I glanced at the time on the clock on my nightstand. "Shoot! I'm going to be late." I grabbed my heels from the bed and hurried down the hall, stopping to hop into each every few steps.

Once I reached the bottom of the staircase, I heard a low whistle.

"You sure do clean up nice," Brock grinned and walked a circle around me.

"Dude, you're a ghost!" Ember called out from the kitchen.

"What's your point?" he shot back, not taking his eyes off me.

"Stop hitting on my mom. She's already spoken for anyway." Ember walked out from the kitchen with a bowl of popcorn in one arm and a bag of assorted candies in the other.

"Movie night?" I asked her.

"Yeah, Aunt Hattie is coming over."

I snickered, "You're having a movie night with Aunt Hattie?"

"Yeah, Aunt Hattie's cool. Plus, she loves horror movies as much as I do."

"Good then. I'm glad she'll be here to keep you company. I won't be late though," I promised, stuffing my wand and cell phone in the small handbag I was taking for the night.

"You do look pretty, mom," Ember said.

"What do you want?" I gave her a suspicious look.

She giggled and widened her eyes, "Nothing. Just trying to pay you a compliment."

Aunt Hattie burst through the front door and I nearly jumped out of my skin.

She paused and gave me a once over, "Fancy."

"I'm going to some party with Lee," I said with about as much enthusiasm as I felt.

"Kiki just left for a party too." She bustled past me.

"Oh great. If Kiki just left, then I'm really going to be late." I raced to the front door and yelled back over my shoulder, "You two have fun tonight. And behave!"

"I always behave!" Ember hollered.

"I was talking to Aunt Hattie!" I pulled the door closed behind me and rushed to my car.

I wasn't sure who was going to be at this party, but I was hopeful there would be at least one person with information.

Even if the bites weren't from a vampire, the police didn't seem to care, and it made me worried for Lara.

I SCROLLED BACK THROUGH MY TEXT MESSAGES TO DOUBLE check that I'd correctly input the address that Lee had sent me into my phone's navigation app. I'd gone far past town and it looked like I was headed in the direction of Craig Baldwin's house. Once I turned onto the road lined with palm trees, I was certain of it. I rolled right past Craig's driveway though and after I passed an expanse of perfectly manicured lawn, I spotted lights. I turned down a long road and began to look for a place to park among the sea of cars that already lined the circular driveway and curled around the giant fountain directly in the center. Once I finally managed to squeeze my car in between two other modest vehicles, I hopped out and hurried to the front entrance of the house. It appeared to be made of charcoal-colored bricks and it was so large and dark that it had a fore-boding presence. I didn't see anyone else scrambling to get inside, which must've meant I was later than I thought.

I could hear soft music coming from inside and I knocked on the door louder than I usually would have. I considered texting Lee to let him know I was there, when the door opened.

"Mayor Valentine," I said with more surprise than I intended.

He offered me a polite smile, "Welcome to my humble abode." He stepped back and allowed me to enter. "Most of the guests are on the patio out back. Can I get you something to drink?"

"Uh, sure," I said, following him through the gorgeous foyer and into the kitchen.

"Wine? A cocktail? Or something less potent?" he asked over his shoulder.

"A glass of wine would be great. Thank you." The truth is, I don't particularly care for wine. But I wanted to blend in with the other guests and still keep a clear head. I figured pretending to enjoy a glass of wine would fit the bill nicely.

"I didn't realize this party was at your home. It's nice of you to host," I attempted to make small talk.

"Yes, well, Rudolph LeBeau has been a dear friend for a long time. I would've offered him space at one of my resorts, but I think he preferred a smaller, more intimate setting." I had completely forgotten that Mayor Valentine owned a few of the resorts down along the coastline. No wonder he could afford a mansion like the one I was standing in.

"Less chance of someone running through in a bikini, too, I suppose."

His lips curved into a smile. "Well, yes, there's that too."

He poured red wine into a glass and handed it to me. "I'll show you back to the patio." I trailed behind him, noting that he carried his own glass of red liquid, though I was certain it was not the same as mine.

He led me through an open pair of glass French doors and out onto a well-lit patio. A patio that was easily as many square feet as my house. A sparkling pool was off to one side and he had a handful of small seating areas placed all around. There was a long table with food near the pool and people were loitering around it, snacking while they chatted. I scanned the crowd for either Lee or Kiki, but I spotted Lee first. I was trying to figure out how to excuse myself, when Rudolph came rushing over and grabbed Mayor Valentine by the arm. I'd been in his store enough times that I recognized him, but I wasn't a frequent enough shopper – or big enough spender - that he'd recognize me.

"Do you mind if I steal him?" Rudolph asked me, the sides of his mustache twitched ever so slightly when he spoke. "There's someone I'd like to introduce him to."

"Of course not," I smiled and made a beeline for Lee who was engrossed in conversation with a very large Valkyrie and another woman in a black shift dress. He didn't even glance in my direction when I approached. Nor did he when I stood awkwardly next to him and received confused looks from both women. I waited for him to pause and take a breath before I jutted my hand out.

"Hello, Shay Graves," I opted to shake hands with the woman in black first.

She shoved a strand of black hair behind her ear and accepted my handshake. "It's nice to meet you. I'm Arabel."

I felt my cheeks flush with embarrassment, "Oh, I'm sorry. I didn't recognize you. I've only seen pictures online and well, you aren't rocking the hat and sunglasses tonight so…"

"It's quite all right," she assured me, patting the top of my hand before she released it.

"I'm Winter," the Valkyrie announced rather abruptly. She thrust her hand at me, and I thought she might shake my arm off. After she let go, I rubbed the top of my sore hand with my thumb.

"Nice to meet you, Winter." I smiled through the throbbing in my hand. "Do you work with Arabel?"

"No. I own a boutique." It seemed her mouth curved downward into a permanent scowl.

"Well, that's wonderful. So, Arabel, I'm surprised I haven't run into you yet. I live on the property just behind the Lettuce Inn."

Arabel drew her eyebrows together, "The cemetery?"

"Yes. Well, I don't live *in* the cemetery. I have a house just across the street from it though. My whole family lives along the lane, actually."

"Oh, yes. I've seen the adorable little row of houses. I have a wonderful view of the cemetery from my room." She seemed to perk up a bit. "I'm almost embarrassed to admit that I haven't left my room much. This hasn't been much of a vacation, to tell you the truth. It's been work, work, work. I'm lucky to get a few hours' sleep at night and a meal that I'm not eating while rushing around Rudolph's studio."

"Do you do these events often?" I asked.

"No, and after this week, I'm reminded why. I'm getting too old for it. I much prefer the boring nine to five routine that allows me to go home to a hot meal and my furry companions." She smiled and I caught a glimpse of her fangs. In the human world, vampires hid them. In a paranormal place like Mystic Key, there was no need and I was still getting used to seeing them so often and unexpectedly.

"When will you be leaving?" I asked.

"Day after tomorrow. And, as much as I love visiting Mystic Key, I am very much looking forward to going home."

"I understand completely," Lee said, finding a way to join the conversation, "I was curious … now, y'all are still staying at the Lettuce Inn even after … you know?"

Arabel frowned and studied him for a full beat. Knowing Lee, he was dying inside but I knew he'd asked the question for me.

"I'm assuming you're referring to the rumors that one of the owners is a suspect in a murder investigation. And, for your information, I chose the word rumor with great intention. Small town gossip is just that and I don't think it's fair to stand here and chinwag about someone behind their back."

Wow. I had never seen Lee speechless before, but he was in that moment. She had really put him in his place, and I was certain he would be crying to me about it later.

"I think my friend here just wanted to make sure you felt safe, is all." I took up for him. After all, I knew he'd only asked the question to see if he could read any thoughts on my behalf.

She let out a small exhale and let her eyes dart back and forth between Lee and me. "I apologize if I was harsh. But I've been the victim of many rumors and I suppose it still strikes a nerve."

"No, I – of course. I'm sorry if I didn't word things correctly," Lee tripped over his words and his voice cracked. He stuck a finger between his neck and the collar of his shirt and gave a little tug.

"It's all right. Truthfully, I haven't had many interactions with any of the sisters, though they seem kind and they've been quite attentive. I only had one small run-in and that was simply an accident."

"Run-in?" The Valkyrie had finally decided to join the conversation.

Arabel rolled her eyes and waved her hand dismissively, "It was nothing really. One of the girls' snakes got out and I found him in my bed."

I fought the urge to snap my head in Lee's direction and I swallowed the lump in my throat. "I didn't know they had snakes."

She tapped her chin with her index finger. "I think just the one girl. The little brunette one. I'm terrible with names."

"Mina." My voice was hoarse and the pit in my stomach sent a wave of nausea over me.

"Yes. Mina! She's quite sweet though. It was just an accident. I believe she said she must've forgotten to secure his cage or something. Anyway, it doesn't matter. It gave me quite a fright, but no harm was done."

"Yeah, I'm sure," Lee said.

"I hate snakes," Winter scrunched up her face and stuck out her lower lip.

"I'm not a fan either," I said.

"Will you excuse me? Rudolph is waving wildly trying to get my attention. It was so lovely meeting you both," Arabel smiled politely and squeezed between Lee and me.

The three of us stood there in silence for an uncomfortably long time before Winter said, "I'm hungry. See ya around." She pushed past Lee and made her way to the food table.

I leaned in close to Lee and lowered my voice, "Did you get anything from her?"

He swallowed hard and sucked in his upper lip, "Okay, first. You owe me. Something big. I don't know what yet. I don't even know when I'll come calling for it. Could be tomorrow, could be next week, could be ten years from now, but you owe me. I made a fool of myself *for* you."

"To be fair, you did a pretty good job making a fool of yourself without my help."

He gave me a dirty look and I held up my hands in defeat.

"I'm kidding. Yes, I know you did it for me and I love you for it."

"All right, now that we're clear. Yes, I did." His eyes darted around behind me and he spoke in a hushed tone. "The snake thing is true. Mina Gratz has a snake. Several, actually."

"Oh, no." I let my head fall back and looked up at the clear night sky. "This is not good, Lee."

"I know. Unfortunately, that's all I was able to get from her, but I think it's enough."

I snapped my head upright and scowled, "It's bad though."

"I mean, yeah, but isn't it better to know you're living next door to a killer than to live in blissful ignorance?"

I shrugged, noncommittal. "I suppose. It still doesn't prove anything though. And it puts the spotlight on all three sisters now too. They all had access to Mina's snakes. The cops like Lara for Brock's murder and I'm sure they can spin it to give her a motive for Craig's too. And now, well, it won't matter that it wasn't vampire venom."

"Shay, have you considered the possibility that she might actually be guilty?"

"Of course."

"Then why are you trying so hard to prove she's not?"

"Because I don't think she is. And because ... because Lara was the only person that supported me when I decided not to move back to Mystic Key."

"You mean after James died?"

"Yeah. My family wanted me to stay so badly, but I just couldn't. I wasn't ready to come back yet. The pressure to stay was so intense that I was almost ready to give in. The day after James' funeral, I was taking a walk and Lara was outside. She invited me in for a cup of tea and we talked for a long time. She told me that if staying away would help me heal, then that's what I needed to do. She said I had to do what was best for myself and my unborn baby. It sort of gave me this renewed conviction and, I don't know ... I've always felt grateful to her for that."

I felt my cell phone buzz in my handbag. "Hang on. I need to make sure that isn't Ember." I pulled out my phone and saw it was a text from Roman.

Roman: My visit with Matthias Sharpe was a bust. He doesn't deal with venomous snakes.

Me: Ok. Aside from some information from Arabel Onassis, I think this party might be too. I'm going to stick around for a bit longer and I'll call you when I get home.

I shoved my phone back in my handbag and told Lee what he'd texted me.

"Oh, well I could've told you that. I know Matthias pretty well. I buy all of my stuff from him."

"I'm starving. I think I'm going to eat a little something and head home."

"So soon?" He seemed surprised.

"I don't even recognize anyone else here." A thought dawned on me. "Wait. Where's Kiki? Have you seen her?"

"I saw her." A grin tugged at the corners of his mouth.

"Let me guess. She already took off with some hunk on her arm?"

"Well, yes, but this particular hunk is a great catch. In fact, he might be a little too vanilla for our Kiki."

I shook my head and pulled my phone back out to text her.

Text me when you get home. I want to know you're safe.

She responded almost immediately.

Will do! We're at Bar Humbug and some of the girls from the salon are here too. I'm safe. Love ya.

"Okay, let's go fill up on expensive finger foods." I looped my arm through Lee's and pulled him toward the food table. "Then I'm going to go home and have a nice, relaxing evening."

$\mathcal{I}$ turned down Shadow Lane and listened to the sound of gravel crunching under the tires. It was still early, the sun barely gone from view, but the moon was so full that light streamed down through the Spanish moss. I'd always loved this part of the lane and the tunnel-like effect it created.

I called Roman to let him know I was almost home and he answered right away.

"Hey, I've been waiting to hear from you. Are you on your way home yet?"

"I am. I just turned onto Shadow Lane."

"Okay. Listen, I started doing a little digging and ended up going down a rabbit hole, but I think I found something. It's a lot to explain, so I'll show you when I get there."

"Sounds good." Matt's house came into view and I saw his police cruiser parked in the driveway. There were lights on all over the house, so I assumed it meant everyone was still up. "Hey, can you meet me at Matt's instead?"

"Sure. Is everything okay?"

"Yeah. I just want to talk with him and if you found something useful then he should hear it too."

I said goodbye to Roman and pulled in behind Paige's minivan. One thing about my family, we aren't great with boundaries. There is a very gray line that we all toe. I turned the knob and let myself in and the sound of my nephew chattering excitedly came from the family room. I headed in the direction of his voice and turned the corner to find a frazzled Paige kneeling on the floor. She had her entire collection of miniature supplies laid out from one end of the family room to the other. MJ rested comfortably on the couch, his video game device in his hands, and it sounded like he was giving his mom a play-by-play of the game he was so enthralled with. I didn't see Matt or Fallon anywhere.

"Hey, Paige." I was almost afraid to interrupt her given the harried look on her face.

Her head snapped up and she had a wild look in her eyes. "I can't find it."

"Can't find what?" I dropped my handbag on the couch next to MJ and knelt down to help her.

"I had the perfect fabric for my Ember doll and now I can't find it." She dumped out another bin filled with various cuts of fabrics and began riffling through them.

"We'll find it." I began sorting the strips with a bit more care than she had taken. "What color is it?"

"It's a brilliant green."

"Brilliant green? I don't know what that means. Light, dark, blueish? Explain it to me like I'm five."

She let out an exasperated breath and sat back on her heels. "I wanted her approval so I could finally finish her doll and it was the perfect color. Now what am I supposed to do?"

"I'm sure Ember won't mind if you choose something else."

"But I already told her about the green!" She nearly shouted. "She's been sitting in the kitchen for the last twenty minutes waiting for me."

"Ember is here?"

"Yeah, Aunt Hattie walked over with her." Paige was distracted again, sorting through a pile of perfectly suitable swatches of green fabric.

"Is Matt around? I was hoping to talk to him."

"In the kitchen." She used her arm to swipe a section of miniature furniture into a pile so she could clear a space for the next bin she was about to dump out.

"Okay. Good luck with your search." I backed away slowly, hoping she wouldn't notice that I had already given up on helping her.

I walked to the kitchen and found Matt, Aunt Hattie, and Ember sitting at the table and playing a game of Uno.

"You can't play a green six on a blue nine," Matt was saying.

"It's a not a six."

"Yes, it is. Look. It has the line there, so you know which number it is." Ember pointed to the giant six on the card.

"No, that's just where some of the color smudged off. It's a nine."

Matt shook his head, but a smile tugged at the corners of his mouth. "Aunt Hattie, stop cheating."

"I'm not. I don't cheat," she huffed.

"Yes, you do," Ember argued. "You cheat all the time."

"You know, if you two don't stop picking on me then I'm not going to play." Aunt Hattie folded her arms over her chest and jutted her chin out.

"Aunt Hattie cheating at Uno again?" I announced my arrival.

Ember turned around in her chair and smiled up at me. "Hey, mom. Your party's already over?"

I pulled out an extra chair and sat down next to her. "It is for me." I noticed my brother was avoiding looking at me, so it was only natural that I call him out on it. "What's up, Matt? You not talking to me or something?"

He scrunched up his brow and pretended to study his cards. "I'm talking to you right now. How was the fashion show thing?"

"Eh. I just went to the after party, but it wasn't really my scene. I was hoping to find you a few new leads, but I came up empty." I decided to hold off on telling him about Mina's snakes for now. I wanted to speak with her myself first. "Speaking of, how come you're at home playing cards right now? I'd think Chief Leach would have you working nonstop until the case is wrapped up."

Matt looked up over his cards at Aunt Hattie and I slid my eyes in her direction.

"You'd better tell her." Aunt Hattie set her mouth in a hard line.

"Remember Morty Mortenson?" Matt asked.

"Of course." I slipped my heels off under the table and leaned back against the chair.

"Well, turns out he was the one who destroyed Brock's car the night he died. We caught him on surveillance leaving the bar and then coming back twenty minutes later. When I went to question him, he confessed. Not for the murder though, but he wasn't on my radar for that anyway."

"I can't say I'm all that surprised. I heard he was pretty angry that Brock never paid him for the work he did."

"He was," Matt nodded and went back to studying the cards in his hand.

"You know that wasn't what I was talking about," Aunt Hattie scowled at him and leaned forward until her bosom rested on the top of the table.

Matt clenched his jaw and closed his eyes for a full beat. When he finally opened them, he set his cards on the table and turned in his seat to face me. "Shay, Chief Leach arrested Lara Gratz this evening."

"What?" I exploded. "On what grounds? It wasn't a vampire that murdered Brock and attacked Craig Baldwin."

He narrowed his eyes and tilted his head to the side, "How do you know that?"

"I have my source," I sniffed. "It doesn't matter. What matters is that you had no reason and no real evidence against her. It's been a witch hunt from day one."

"Vampire hunt," Ember said.

"Yeah, vampire hunt. Unless there's something you're not telling me, I really don't understand why the focus has been solely on Lara this whole time."

Matt rolled his neck from one side to the other. "Shay, we found out that the Gratzes have snakes. Mina, specifically, but that's irrelevant. If it wasn't vampire venom, then it was certainly snake venom. Furthermore, Lara had problems with both victims. Big, public problems."

"This is unbelievable. What about her alibi?"

He smirked and rolled his eyes. "You mean her sister? That's not an alibi, Shay. It wasn't even true, either. The guest that's staying at the inn, Arabel Onassis, mentioned seeing Gretchen in the communal living room there the night Brock was murdered. She'd gone down to the kitchen for her nightly drink and had a brief conversation with Gretchen at a little after ten. Which, if you recall, is the time Gretchen said her and her sister were out for a walk to cool off."

"Maybe she had the time wrong." I could hear the defeat in my own voice.

"I don't think she did." Matt reached over and placed his hand over mine. "Look, Shay, I know you don't want her to be guilty, but we do have some solid circumstantial evidence."

I looked down at my lap, searching my brain for any possible avenues we might've overlooked.

MJ came bounding into the kitchen with Roman following close behind.

"Roman, hey." Matt sounded surprised to see him.

"Oh, I forgot to mention that Roman would be coming by," I said.

"Sorry to intrude." Roman walked around the table and pulled out an empty chair. He didn't waste any time opening his laptop.

Matt looked back and forth between the two of us. "What's going on?"

"Roman said he found something interesting," I said.

"Aunt Shay, can I show you my game now?" MJ was standing next to me and the hopeful look on his face wasn't one I could say no to.

"Sure, buddy." I pulled him onto my lap and strained to listen to Roman and Matt's conversation over the noise coming from MJ's game.

"So, I was curious about the purple venom since it's nothing anyone around here has seen before," Roman started.

"I have," Aunt Hattie interjected.

"When?" Matt's voice had a suspicious tone to it.

Aunt Hattie had an annoyed look on her face. "I told you, a fella died around here a long time ago. We all thought it was a vampire attack. But it had that same purple stuff that Brock's wounds did."

"And they couldn't test for stuff like they can now," Ember added. "Aunt Hattie was telling me about it tonight."

"Okay, so aside from that murder …" Roman gave Aunt Hattie a sidelong glance, "no one has seen it before. I decided to search the paraweb to see if there have been any reports of something similar."

Matt stood and moved around the table to stand behind Roman.

"I only had time to search back to the early nineteen hundreds, but since then there have been over two hundred cases reported."

There was a collective gasp around the table from everyone except MJ. He looked up briefly, but immediately went back to his game. "Are you watching, Aunt Shay?"

"Yes, sweetie. I'm watching." I glanced down at the screen and saw a female character descending from the sky and into what appeared to be a village.

"Most of the victims didn't make it," Roman continued, "but around twenty survived the attack. Of those twenty, only three ever regained any memories related to the attack. One man says he met a woman in a bar and took her back to his house. Another said he remembered being suspended in the air and feeling like he was taped up. He said he wasn't able to move. Something was keeping him immobile. He also reported hearing a weird clicking noise, but he'd lost vision during that time. I couldn't find anything about the third man and he's since passed."

"I'm Athena," MJ said.

"What's that, buddy?" I looked down at his game which now showed two female characters and a range of onlookers in the background.

"I'm Athena. You know, the goddess? Every level you get to

be a different god or goddess. On this one, I'm Athena and I have to defeat this other lady. She's been talking trash about me."

I chuckled and ruffled the hair on the top of his head. "Oh, yeah? And what's she been saying?"

"So, we're looking at a suspect with a very long lifespan." Matt had his brow knit together in thought.

"Or an immortal," Roman said.

MJ squirmed in my lap. "Well, my character is the one that taught her everything and now she's saying that she's better than me. So, Athena warned her not to talk bad about the gods and she challenged me to a contest. If I win, I get to give her any punishment I want. Well, I don't, the game does, but it's all from … what's it called?"

"Mythology?"

"Yeah, mythology."

"I know Athena, but I'm not sure I'm familiar with this story," I said.

"We've already ruled out vampires," Roman said.

"See, look." MJ leaned back so I could over his shoulder better. "We have to battle by weaving a tapestry." He jabbed his thumbs against the buttons, and I watched the two characters on the screen furiously began weaving.

"Yeah, the venom came back no match for vampires," Matt agreed.

Roman turned in his chair and looked up at him. "And from what I've been able to learn, snakes aren't all that likely either."

"Yes!" MJ exclaimed, nearly jumping from my lap. "I won. Did you see me, Aunt Shay?"

"I did. Great job, buddy."

"Now comes the fun part." He giggled and pounded at the buttons and I watched the screen as one of the characters transformed from a woman into a spider. I felt a sense of dread forming in the pit of my stomach.

"See, Athena turned her into a spider because she was bragging about being so good at weaving. Cool, huh?"

I nodded, trying to find the words, and swallowed the lump in my throat.

"Shay?" Roman must have seen the strange look on my face.

"Spider," I choked out the word.

"Where?" Matt started searching the ceiling.

"No," I shook my head hard, trying to clear it. "It's not a vampire or a snake. It's a spider."

"Well, that's just great." Aunt Hattie dropped her hand down on the table. "I haven't had to deal with one of those mean old things for years."

"You know about spiders?" I was shocked.

"Sure. They're technically called Arachne. It was the name of the dumb woman from the story about Athena. They take human form, but they can transform whenever they please."

"Why didn't you mention this before?" Matt sounded shocked.

"I forgot about 'em." She shrugged. "I haven't seen one in so long I just plumb forgot."

"How are we going to figure out who in this town is an Arachne then?" Roman asked.

I swallowed hard and cleared my throat. "I think … I think I already know."

CHAPTER SEVENTEEN

"*B*ut it just doesn't make any sense," I shook my head, trying to make sense of things. "She's a vampire."

"Who, Shay?" Matt was growing impatient, the muscle in his jaw twitched.

"Arabel Onassis. I saw her fangs just tonight. And she had the Gratzes have a supply of golden blood for her."

What sounded like shouting came from somewhere outside, and both Matt and Roman dashed toward the front door. I scooped MJ up and placed him in Ember's lap. "Stay here and keep MJ with you," I told her, before running after them.

"Shay!" Aunt Hattie called out after me, but I pretended not to hear her.

I made it out onto the porch just in time to see Roman and Matt on their way down to my Uncle Burl's house. He was standing just to the side of his house, in his underwear, and hollering curses to himself.

In my haste, I'd forgotten to put my shoes back on and winced and yelped as I tiptoed across the gravel road to reach Uncle Burl's place.

Matt and Roman stood with their backs to me and by the looks of their relaxed posture, I assumed this was a typical Uncle Burl emergency. In other words, it was no emergency at all.

"What's going on?" I called out to him.

"Freakin' idiots, that's what!" He stood behind some large device that he had shoved into a muddy hole in the ground.

Roman leaned over and said, "It's a pump."

"Uncle Burl, what are you doing with a sewage pump?" Matt asked.

"Cleaning up their mess!" He turned around and threw his arm out in the direction of the Lettuce Inn. "Their sewage line is connected to ours and something burst a pipe. Now I got this weird stuff bubbling up all over my lawn."

"Gross," I muttered.

"It is." He shut off the pump and bent down to examine something on the ground. His eyes grew so big that I thought they might pop out of his head. He let out a low whistle and looked up at Matt. "Hey, son, you got some kind of strainer?"

"For what?" Matt had a repulsed look on his face.

"I think this is golden blood here mixed in with the sewage. I might be able to strain it out and resell it."

I gagged involuntarily, "Don't you dare."

Roman took a few hesitant steps forward. "Wait. If there's golden blood in their sewage system, that means someone is just dumping it down the toilet."

"Yes, it does." Matt's expression hardened. "Shay, are you one hundred percent sure you saw fangs?"

"I am."

Uncle Burl scoffed and lit a cigar that he'd pulled from somewhere. "If someone can afford golden blood, you think they can't afford some dental work?"

"So, she's been masquerading as a vampire for who knows how long," Roman said.

I glanced up at the Lettuce Inn and noticed a light on in a room on the top floor. "It's a good way not to get caught."

Matt was already on his cell phone and talking hurriedly to dispatch. Once he was done, he started toward his house. "Roman, can you take Shay back to my house and make sure everyone stays inside with the doors locked?"

"On it." Roman nodded.

"What about me? Am I in danger?" Uncle Burl took a long drag off his cigar. "Do I need to watch out for someone?"

"As long as you're running around in your skivvies, I'm sure they'll be watching out for you," Matt called back before he launched into a full sprint.

I started for the gravel road when I felt Roman's arm hit my legs from behind. My knees buckled and suddenly I was being lifted into the air and carried like a baby. His shoes crunched against the gravel and I looked up at him in surprise.

"You're not wearing shoes. Figured I'd help you get across the lane." He smiled down at me.

Once we crossed the road, he set me down gently and I straightened my dress. "Thanks."

He put an arm around me while we walked back to Matt's house and I could hear the sirens in the distance.

"That was fast," I said.

A pair of headlights turned down the road and I squinted and held a hand up to shield my eyes. "Must be Kiki."

When the car continued past Kiki's house, I felt a wave of panic wash over me. It pulled to a screeching halt and I heard rocks pelt the underside of the bumper. After a moment, the headlights shut off and Lee emerged from the driver's side.

"Lee? What are you doing here?"

He held up one hand and placed the other on his chest like he was trying to catch his breath.

"Lee, you didn't run here. You've been driving. Stop being theatrical."

"Shay, please. I am never theatrical." He stood upright and pulled down on the bottom of his suit jacket. "Anyway, this is a serious matter. I think I know what's going on around here. I know who the killer is." He lifted his chin and smiled proudly.

"We do too," I said.

His face fell.

"Sorry, detective, but you're a little late. We know it's Arabel Onassis. Don't you hear the sirens? The police are already on their way to pick her up."

He stuck out his lower lip in a pout. "That's always my luck. A day late and a dollar short."

"Aw, Lee." I threw my arm around him and gave him a little squeeze. "That was pretty smart of you to figure it out. It took a whole table full of Graves and one Daniels to do it."

He grinned and put his arm around my shoulders. "You're right. I am smart."

"I don't mean to interrupt, but we really should get back to the house like Matt requested," Roman said.

We walked along the grass until we reached the front of Matt's house and I heard a shriek from somewhere in the graveyard.

I froze and whispered, "That sounded like Kiki." Without thinking twice, I spun around on my heels and hurried back down the road toward where the sound had come from.

"Shay, wait!" Roman called out after me. I didn't stop to wait for him to catch up. If my sister was in trouble, I needed to help her.

CHAPTER EIGHTEEN

I heard another shriek and this time I was able to pinpoint exactly where it had come from. I spotted Brock standing in the middle of the graveyard with a terrified look on his face. He saw me and shouted, "Stay back!"

No sooner had he said it than I felt something hit me in the stomach. It took my breath away and I looked down to see a ball of white strands stuck to my dress. I followed the single strand back to its source until it disappeared into the darkness.

"Shay!" I heard Kiki cry.

I grabbed at the silk and ripped it away from my dress and raced into the darkness.

I could hear Roman shouting protests, but I needed to get Kiki safe.

Brock stepped in front of me, but I sailed right through him and continued until I saw my sister. She was wrapped in a spiderweb that extended around the tree to keep her in place.

"Shay, run! Go get help!" She screamed.

"I am the help!" I yelled back. At that moment, the biggest spider I'd ever seen peeked its head out from the other side of the tree. It raised its giant legs, one at a time, and moved out from its hiding spot.

"Oh, sweet sorcery," I muttered under my breath.

Kiki screamed again and shut her eyes tight. I could feel Roman behind me now.

"I don't have my wand," I whispered. "It's in my handbag at Matt's."

"I'm not leaving you here to go get it," he whispered back.

"Then what are we supposed to do?"

His brow was scrunched together, and I could see the concentration in his eyes.

"Um … Miss Onassis?" I called out. "Can we just talk for a minute?"

She tilted her head, as if considering my question.

"I'm not your enemy. In fact, I couldn't care less that you killed Brock and went after Craig."

Brock gasped and I could see the hurt in his eyes. I'd have to explain to him later that I was only trying to buy time.

"You're lying," the giant spider finally spoke, but her voice was a low hissing sound.

"No, I'm not. In fact, I have a theory about why you did it. I'd love to know if I was correct. So, can you tell me why you killed Brock?"

The spider took a step forward and I braced myself, but she didn't continue. "It's just what I do. After I mate, I kill the male. It's not personal." She let out a low hiss and I felt the hair raise on my arms. "I only choose males that are deserving though. I'm very careful about that."

"Hey. What's that supposed to mean?" Brock grumbled, crossing his arms over his chest.

I sucked in a breath and let it out, willing myself to sound convincing. "I get it. You choose the chauvinists, the playboys, the narcissists. The men who don't respect you."

"They don't respect any woman. The world is better off without them. Since I must mate and kill, this is a fabulous compromise, don't you think?"

"Sure," I cleared my throat, "but what about my sister? She's innocent."

"She saw me leaving the bar with a new mate. I tried to be careful, but she recognized me. I could tell by the look in her eyes that she knew."

"I won't tell anyone. Just let me go!" Kiki struggled against the web and Arabel shook with laughter.

"This has gone too far, Arabel. I'm sorry for your ... plight, I guess? But you can't kill innocent people. Especially not my sister."

I heard movement in the grass next to me and Roman took a single leap before a thick web of silk shot forward, hitting him square in the chest. He fell to the ground with a hard thud.

"I thought we were friends. Why would you do that to a friend?" he spoke in a soothing, gentle voice and I was thoroughly confused.

The spider cocked its head to the side and let out what almost sounded like a sigh. That's when it hit me. Roman was trying to use his druid magic on the Arachne.

"It's all going to be all right. I won't hurt you," he was saying, as he slowly stood back up.

The spider seemed to relax, lowering herself a little closer to the ground, but the movement frightened Kiki and she belted out another ear-splitting scream. The spider jumped back up and hissed.

"Sorry," Kiki said through tears.

The spider started toward us and Roman and I split up, each ducking behind a headstone while she shot strands of silk at us.

"I need my wand!" I yelled to him.

I saw a streak of orange darting through the dark, weaving in between headstones.

Be careful. She's fast, I warned Steve.

Need I remind you I have cat-like reflexes? I spotted him bounding toward me and he took one final leap into my arms.

Good point. Listen, I don't have my wand. I left it in my handbag at Matt's house. Can you get it?

He raised his chin to look up at me and I read the judgment in his eyes. *I know. What kind of a witch am I?*

I think we both know the answer to that one. He sprung from my arms and dashed through the dark in the direction of Matt's house.

The Arachne shot strings of silk after him, but he was right —he was impressively fast and agile. When he was finally out of view, she turned her attention back to me.

"Shay? Where are ya?" Aunt Hattie's voice called out from somewhere close by. Crap. I couldn't let the Arachne get her. I stood and whistled to get the spider's attention. Which I managed to do just long enough to see Aunt Hattie and Lee both drop to their knees behind a rather large statue of an angel.

"If you two are here, who went to let the cops know we need help?" I yelled.

My question was met with silence for a solid thirty seconds. "Ember was going to call Matt," Lee finally said.

I ducked back down behind the headstone and contemplated my next move.

"She's going to try to take you out first, Shay. She thinks you're the biggest threat," Lee said in a hushed tone.

In spite of the circumstances, I actually laughed. Clearly, the Arachne had not met my Aunt Hattie before.

"Works for me!" I yelled, popping up from behind my hiding spot like a jack-in-the-box.

The Arachne began to shoot webs at me in rapid succession and I dove to avoid them the best I could. A few moments later, I saw a spray of magic fly through the air and its green aura settled over the spider. She continued to try to shoot strands of silk, but nothing appeared. After a few frustrated minutes, she ran for me instead. I screamed and weaved in and out of headstones, trying to figure out exactly what my next move should be.

"Shay, hold still!" Aunt Hattie yelled.

"Oh, sure. And get eaten by a giant spider?" I looked back over my shoulder and watched as the spider placed one long leg after another over the headstones.

"Trust me!" Aunt Hattie ordered.

I let out a deep breath and stopped short of the tree Kiki was stuck to. The spider was closing in on me, her long legs poised in the air and her mouth open. She was so close I could see the purple venom dripping from her mouth. I was too afraid to scream, but I felt fear coursing through me. A burst of white magic enveloped her, and she let out a anguished hiss. The magic sucked her in and, before I had time to process, she was so small I wouldn't have been able to see her if not for the magic glowing around her. She dropped to the ground and froze, stunned. I promptly lifted my leg and stomped down on her with my barefoot. I felt her squish on the bottom of my heel and I let out a disgusted shriek.

"Shay? Did you just step on a spider with your barefoot? That is disgusting!" Kiki admonished.

A parade of running feet was drawing closer and I saw Matt

leading the herd. He had his gun drawn and he stopped and looked around frantically.

"She's gone." Aunt Hattie placed one hand on top of the headstone and the other on Lee's head to help her climb to her feet.

Lee popped up a second later and used his hands to straighten up his ruffled hair.

"What do you mean gone? Where did she go?" Chief Leach finally reached the front of the group of police officers. He placed his hands on his hips and had a mean scowl on his face.

A few police officers ran over and began to free Kiki from the tree. I waited until she was down and threw my arms around her. "Are you okay?"

She nodded into my shoulder and I pulled back to look at her. "Your makeup's a mess." I attempted a joke.

She smiled and let out a little laugh. I put my arm around her and led her over to join everyone else.

"Is someone going to tell me where the spider lady went?" Chief Leach was tapping his foot.

"Shay squished her," Aunt Hattie said matter-of-factly.

"With her barefoot," Kiki grimaced.

"You four took down an Arachne?" Chief Leach looked skeptical. "I'm not sure I buy that."

"Well, you'd better," Lee matched Chief Leach's stance. "You're lucky we did your job for you."

"And who are you?" Leach glared up at Lee.

"It doesn't matter who I am. It matters who we are. And we, sir, are the witches of Shadow Lane." Lee popped his hip out and bopped Leach on the nose.

I snorted out a laugh. "Lee, you aren't a witch."

"And you don't live here either," Kiki said.

He shot us a glare and moved to stand behind Aunt Hattie, "Y'all are mean sometimes, you know that?"

"I'll tell ya what happened," Aunt Hattie said, "I shrunk the spider and Shay stepped on it. Evidence is probably on the bottom of her foot. That's the long and short of it." She turned and began waddling toward her house.

"Where are you going?" Matt asked.

"Home." She waited until she was a few steps away before I heard her mutter. "Dummy. Where else would I be going?"

Matt rolled his eyes and placed a gentle hand on Kiki's arm. "We should probably get you to the hospital. Just to make sure you're okay."

She nodded and let Matt lead her back toward his house.

The crowd of police dispersed, and I stood with Roman and Lee in the middle of the graveyard. "Thank you both for your help. I need to go grab Ember – and my shoes – but after that, I'd like to buy you both a piece of pie for your trouble."

"Helping you is never any trouble," Roman smiled and gave me a quick wink. "But I'll never say no to pie."

"I'm in too," Lee sniffed. "So long as you apologize for saying I'm not one of you."

I chuckled and looped my arm through his. "I apologize for saying that the angel of Bradford Street is not a witch of Shadow Lane. You can be an honorary one though, how about that?"

"Thank you. That's all I ask." He lifted his chin and smiled.

CHAPTER NINETEEN

"*I* think you're really starting to get the hang of it," I said, offering Ember a small clap.

"I know!" She bounced up on her tiptoes with excitement. She pointed her wand back at the wooden spoon and moved it in a methodically, clockwise motion. The spoon mimicked her movements, stirring the batter.

I watched from a chair in the kitchen, a cup of hot coffee resting between my hands. "You know, you could always just use the electric mixer too."

She made a noise and shook her head. "Mom, what's the point of being a witch if I'm just going to use modern conveniences for everything. I want to use my magic. And, not to be rude, but you could take a lesson from me."

I snickered. "I beg your pardon?"

"I mean it. You hardly ever use your magic. You even have a wand now, but you still don't." She stopped stirring and turned around to face me. "What's the deal?"

"There is no deal." I stared down into my coffee mug.

"Don't let her off the hook that easily." Steve wandered into the kitchen, brushing his side against the cupboards.

"You stay out of this." I narrowed my eyes at him.

"Oops. Looks like we've struck a nerve," he mused.

"No. There's no nerve. You two stop trying to make something out of nothing. It's just that I didn't use my magic for so long … I'm rusty. I asked Aunt Hattie if she'd give us both lessons."

"Oh, that sounds fun." She smiled brightly.

"It does not sound fun in the least," Steve said.

"Well you're not invited anyway." Ember plopped down on the floor next to him and stroked his back. "Hey mom, how come I don't have a familiar yet?"

"I've been wondering the same, actually. I'm sure they'll show up soon enough though."

"Frankly, I'm glad they haven't. I'm not looking forward to having to set another being straight about who is in charge around here," Steve said, "it took me long enough to train you two."

I took a drink of my coffee and set it down on the table. "Then there's always the possibility that you wind up with a familiar as charming and easy going as Steve," I said in a sarcastic tone.

"Unlikely." He yawned and placed his chin on Ember's knee.

"That Brock guy is gone for good now, right?" she asked.

"He is. And I can't say I'm going to miss him. The other good news is that Lara Gratz isn't being harassed by the police anymore and Craig Baldwin is recovering well. Matt said he went home from the hospital yesterday."

"Get your dirty paws off my witch." An unfamiliar voice came from the window. I jumped from my chair, knocking it to the floor, and saw the face of a goat peaking up over the open windowsill.

"Who are you?" I asked.

"I'm Bruce," he said, as if I should know that already.

"Uh … hi, Bruce. What can I help you with?"

"Well, you can open the door and let me in for starters."

"And why would we do a dumb thing like that?" Steve asked.

"Because that's my witch," he said again.

"Me?" Ember pointed to her chest. "I'm your witch?"

"Yes, ma'am." He bopped his head up and down.

"Oh no. No, no, no. We cannot have some disgusting farm animal living in this house." Steve leapt to his feet.

"Steve, be nice," I scolded.

"I *am* being nice. This is me, being nice."

"Listen, I don't want any problems with you, pal, but I'm not going to take your crap either," Bruce said.

Steve leapt onto the kitchen table and from there to the windowsill. Less than a second later, Bruce froze and then disappeared.

Ember and I looked at each other and then back to the spot where Bruce had been.

"Bruce?" I called out.

"Where did he go?" Ember asked.

Steve leaned forward and looked out the window. "He's just laying there."

"Steve! What did you do?" I asked, hurrying to the back door.

"Did you kill him?" Ember hissed.

I threw open the back door just in time to see Bruce climbing to his feet.

"Oh my goddess, are you okay? What happened?" I asked.

"Oh, yes, I'm fine. It happens all the time."

"What does?" Ember asked.

"I faint. I'm a fainting goat. When I get scared or surprised, I faint." Bruce lifted his chin and looked back and forth between the two of us.

"A… a fainting goat … for a familiar." I was having a hard time wrapping my brain around how exactly that would work.

"You got it." Bruce said, trotting past Ember and I and heading for the open door. "So, where am I sleeping?" He hopped up the stairs and walked inside, leaving Ember and I staring at each other dumbfounded.

"He can't stay in the house … can he?" I asked.

"I don't know." She shrugged. "You're the mom. You tell me."

"I know, but I have no idea. I've never been around a goat before." I whispered.

"Would you like my opinion?" Steve asked.

"No." Ember and I answered in unison.

"Okay. Well, I have no idea how to care for a goat, but we'll figure it out," I said.

"We always do." She smiled and turned to head back into the house.

And she was right. One way or another, we always figured it out.

THANK YOU

Thank you so much for reading! The Witches of Shadow Lane is an ongoing series. You can see a full list of books by the author on the following page.

One final note … if you'd like to be notified of new releases, giveaways, and special deals, you can sign up for my newsletter on my website at www.mistybane.com. Not an email person? You can also keep track of my new releases by following me:

On Facebook

On Bookbub

On Amazon

ALSO BY MISTY BANE

BLACKWOOD BAY WITCHES MYSTERY SERIES

Haunted and Hexed (Book 1)

Bad Magic and the Big Top (Book 2)

Phantoms in High Fidelity (Book 3)

Broomsticks and Bones (Book 4)

Payback's a Witch (Book 5)

Blackwood Bay Witches Mystery Shorts

On a Witch and a Spell (Prequel Novelette)

One Spell of a Time

THE WITCHES OF SHADOW LANE

Witchy Business (Book 1)

Witchy Orders (Book 2)

Witchy Secrets (Book 3)

Would you like to be notified about new releases and special offers?

You can sign up for my newsletter here. I promise not to spam you with sales-y emails. I *will* share new releases and giveaways though.

Not an email person? You can follow me on Facebook and you can also join my Facebook Reader Group here.

Website

Facebook

Newsletter Sign Up

ABOUT THE AUTHOR

Misty Bane is a Pacific Northwest native currently living somewhere between the mountains and the beach with her husband, three children, and golden retriever, Lou. She often fantasizes about living in a world where she could clean the house and whip up a four-course meal with just a twirl of her finger.

Keep up with Misty by following her on social media. To be notified of new releases and special discounts, join her newsletter list. She has a strict anti-spam policy and you will never receive anything you didn't sign up for.

You can also join her Facebook Reader Group.

Or Email: misty@mistybane.com

Made in the USA
Las Vegas, NV
14 August 2021